Special thanks to
Larriane, Carol, Dawne, and Scott

Books by MK Scott

The Painted Lady Inn Mysteries Series

Murder Mansion

Drop Dead Handsome

Killer Review

Christmas Calamity

Death Pledges a Sorority

Caribbean Catastrophe

Weddings Can Be Murder

The Talking Dog Detective Agency Series

A Bark in the Night

Requiem for a Rescue Dog Queen

Requiem for a Rescue Dog Queen

The Talking Dog Detective Agency

by

MK Scott

Chapter One

THE SUNLIGHT PAINTED the lake with a golden shimmer. Nala leaned back in her boat seat as her handsome companion expertly guided the craft toward the pier. He'd mentioned reservations at a lakeside restaurant that had received a stellar review in The Indy Star newspaper. The thought of the renowned grilled rainbow trout had her mouth watering, or maybe it was her date. She glanced back to the tall figure at the wheel. With his broad shoulders and thick, wavy, dark hair, he was almost movie-star handsome, which caused her a momentary pang. What was he doing with her, a preschool teacher turned private eye? She'd never stop traffic with her cute nose and average figure.

Forget about it and enjoy the moment. Her hair streamed behind her as the boat picked up speed. Even though it had been a hot Indian Summer day, going this fast on the water chilled her. The windbreaker she brought just in case would solve the issue but would cover up the flirty top she'd donned for the date. Should she be comfortable or becoming?

A loud noise interrupted before she could decide. The lake remained empty and calm, except for the wake behind the boat. Using her flat hand as a sun shield for her eyes, she peered toward the shore to figure out who might be playing the same trio of notes repeatedly. No one on the shoreline, which only deepened the mystery. It sounded so familiar. In an *aha* moment, she realized it was her phone. Unfortunately, the realization forced her to open her eyes in her dark bedroom.

The red numerals on her clock indicated it was one-thirty in the morning. It was too late or too early for anyone to call. The sound stopped when she realized the tune had been the one she assigned to Karly, her best friend. Karly would only call her this late if it was an emergency. A cold canine nose touched her hand as she reached for her phone on the nightstand.

"Go back to sleep, Max. It doesn't involve you."

Even though it was dark and Max was a black German shepherd mix, she would have sworn the dog cocked his head and gave her an *oh, really* look. The damp nose disappeared with the sound of dog nails on the wood floor as Max settled on the floor. She could hear him mutter under his breath, "We'll see."

Yeah, dealing with a talking dog could be problematic at times. Her fingers found the phone which now had a glowing dot on the dashboard for notifications. Before she could call back, the phone rang again, vibrating in her hand. Karly again.

"Why in the world would you be calling me in the middle of the night?"

Her friend's breathless voice gasped out. "We need your help!"

"We?" Her friend had never been a steady *we* since she tended to form relationships with men that were strictly *me* people. She usually figured it out after a few dates when she sometimes ended up splitting the bill or paying for everything since her companion conveniently forgot his wallet. Karly couldn't afford a love life.

"Fiona and me. I'm at her house, and the police just left. They aren't taking this seriously."

"Not taking what seriously? Did you need to call me in the middle of the night?" No need to add she'd ruined a perfectly wonderful dream, which was about as close as she got to romance, lately.

"I had to call you. There was no one else I could depend on. It's important someone in authority knows what's going on."

If she were trying to reach someone in authority, she'd misdialed. The only thing Nala had control over was Max and her own life, and neither one ever did what she wanted. "You called me as an authority?"

"No, not really. I thought you could pass it on to your father, who, as a captain on the police force, could exercise some control in the matter. Maybe give the officer who blew us off a good talking to."

She shoved up into a sitting position and turned on the lamp, even though it made her wince with the sudden explosion of light. Max shot her a disdainful look and padded out of the room, possibly for a darker sleeping area. "You haven't told me anything. Who's Fiona? What happened that you had to call the police?"

Karly gave an audible inhale before starting. "Fiona Bridgewater, she's the woman I told you about who inherited all the money and started a personal no-kill dog shelter on the county line."

A slight memory surfaced of her friend gushing about a lucky woman who had a boatload of money and was constructing her own giant kennel for homeless dogs. Karly met her because the woman had relieved the shelter of twenty dogs at one time. She usually took the handicapped and elderly dogs, the ones that had the least chance of adoption. Nala remembered thinking at the time if she'd inherited a boatload of money she'd pay off her credit cards and take a luxury cruise.

"I remember."

Karly gave a little sniff, an indication she was very upset and had been crying or the autumn pollen was getting to her, possibly both.

"Well, she built her kennel, which is really nice. Very state of the art. It's like those stables for thoroughbreds."

"Karly," she gently reminded, knowing her friend could get wound up about kennels the way some women did movie stars. "What happened?"

"Yeah, that. Someone has taken exception to Fiona's personal dog sanctuary."

"That might be understandable, having twenty dogs barking constantly." Whenever Max decided to go into a full-out barking frenzy, it got old very fast. At least her dog understood her when she demanded he stop.

"Oh no, it's not like that. She's out in the middle of nowhere. Fiona bought forty acres and stuck her kennel in the middle of it next to the old house. You need to drive down a long stretch to reach it. There's no zoning, which is why she purchased the property. A quarter horse farm, about a half mile away is her closest neighbor."

"Okay." Her lips twisted as she tried to figure out what caused her friend to call. "Why did you call the police?"

"The idiots who have been harassing her returned. She thinks it is just teenagers out on a lark, but this time they went too far. I remember your dad saying something about the police couldn't do anything without a chain of evidence. I was trying to establish that chain."

"In the middle of the night?"

"Fiona and I were working on a campaign to raise money for my shelter and the need to neuter their pets to prevent more homeless cats and dogs. Time got away from us since we were both in the zone."

Even though her friend couldn't see it, she smirked, knowing very well what her friend could be like. "What's been happening?"

"She received threatening phone calls about silencing her dogs permanently."

She could see how that would be upsetting to a dog lover. "Did she try to star 69 to find out who it was?"

"Blocked number."

"That could be problematic. Anything else?"

"There was a note placed on her car, describing what they'd do to the dogs. It was graphic." Karly made a shivery groan into the phone.

"What happened to the note?"

"The police took it, but I managed to snap a shot of it for you."

She really rather would have had the actually note. At least that way Elvin could have lifted prints from it and have some of his borderline legal associates run them. No need to mention that more serious crimes, such as murder and extortion, would take precedence over nasty notes about dogs. "Thanks. You called the police about that in the middle of the night?"

"No. It was the fire."

"Fire!" The news started her neurons firing on all cylinders. "Are you okay?" Then she remembered the rescues. "The dogs?"

"Yes. Thank goodness Fiona spared no expense with the kennel. The perimeter alarm went off, which was something she had installed recently, startling us. We ran outside and saw the flames by the kennel. Fiona had fire extinguishers, which put out the blaze. I insisted we call the police. They came. Told us we had nothing to worry about since the kennel was concrete and had a slate roof. It would have to be an intense fire to touch it. Officer Daylen took the report and the note. In my opinion, Daylen didn't seem too concerned about the phone calls since Fiona had no record of them, only her word. Probably wrote it off as crazy dog ladies starting a fire for attention."

"Hmm." She stalled, wondering if Karly might be right. Her father had related some bizarre tales around the dining room table on occasion, everything from spurned lovers being locked outside in their birthday suits to adults dressed up as Indy 500 drivers holding up a Dairy Queen and requesting payment in dilly bars. It might not be as heartless as Karly thought to take their complaint with a grain of salt. After all, both were awake and dressed, which at that time of night could be viewed as suspicious. "I'm sure it's not that. Officers are trained not to show too many emotions."

"Ha! He showed emotion all right. It was no secret we were wasting his time."

"Everyone has good and bad days. Maybe he wasn't at the top of his game. What do you want me to do for you besides complain to my dad?"

"Well," Karly hesitated.

Nala rolled her eyes knowing whatever the request was she wouldn't especially like it. "Spit it out."

"I thought you and your wonderful detective dog could come out and look for clues."

"It's still o' dark-thirty, if you haven't noticed."

"I thought Max could question the dogs, while the incident is still fresh in their minds."

Apparently, her friend had more confidence in her dog's ability than she did. "It doesn't work like that. Max pretty much avoids other dogs. I don't ever remember him having a conversation with one. Now and then he senses something from body language, and he does get info from smell."

"Bring him out and at least let him do that. I've told Fiona so much about him that she wants to meet him. I think it will help get her mind off this awful situation."

Even though she had no desire to do so, Nala knew she'd end up driving to some unknown destination. Karly had such a soft heart. "Where are you?"

"It's near Tipton, off one of those country roads. Once you get to Tipton, call me, and Fiona will walk you through getting here."

"Okay." Nala was already up and searching through her closet for something that struck the right balance between private eye and preschool teacher. Her sudden decision to quit her preschool job left her school with no certified teacher. She'd agreed to sub until they found someone. It wasn't a bad deal, since at present she had no cases. It provided some money but not the amount she'd earned as a regular teacher for doing the exact same things. "Talk to you soon."

"Thanks, Nala. You're a saint."

Easy touch, gullible, anxious to please, all of those might fit, but not *saint*. If she had any saintly attributes, she'd not be resenting her impromptu trip in the wee hours. After she dressed and pulled on her shoes, she whistled for Max.

"Guess what? We get to do a middle of the night investigation, courtesy of Karly." She expected some whining since her pooch never withheld his feelings.

"Yippee! Wow! Wow." He shook his head. "Sorry about that last bit. I just sounded like a yodeling basenji in my enthusiasm. What's the case?"

"Not sure if it's a case or not, but there's a local woman who built her own dog shelter and is getting threats for doing so."

"Fiona," Max added as he pushed up from his place on the couch and stretched.

"How do you know her? Were you listening to my call?"

He wiggled his shoulders then shot her a doggy grin. "While I may have many superb talents, hearing what is being said on the other end of the phone while asleep is not one of them. Fiona Bridgewater is the canine answer to Daddy Warbucks from *Annie*. She sweeps into a shelter and takes all the hard luck dogs home to endless T-bones and beef scented bubble baths."

"I doubt the dogs have it that good. Who'd want a beef scented bubble bath? Yuck."

"Don't knock it until you try it."

"When have you ever had beef scented bubble bath?"

He hung his head. "My companion is too miserly to buy me my own bubble bath."

Max, due to Karly's influence, insisted on referring to her as his companion or business partner. At times, it both amused and irritated her. "Grab something to eat and drink since we're heading out. And what's more, I've never seen any meat scented bubble bath anywhere."

Her pet headed to the kitchen for a quick drink and begrudging bite of kibble. He managed to talk around a mouth full of dog food, dribbling it on the floor. "You can buy bacon soap online."

How would he know that? It was enough that Max had favorite shows he liked to watch, but she did not even want to consider he could be surfing the net using her computer or phone. It was probably her phone since it had voice commands. "End of subject. We're on the clock. If I get this done in a timely fashion, we'll both be able to grab some Z's. If not, I'll drop you off on my way to preschool."

Max joined her at the door. "Preschool. Children. I'd love to go with you. It's so much fun playing the running and screaming game. I make the short humans run in a circle, waving their hands, and screaming for all their worth."

"Which is why you're never allowed at preschool. Besides, little Kellum is allergic to dogs." Nala flicked on the porch light and waited for her dog to exit before locking the door.

They strolled to her vintage Volkswagen Beetle as Max continued to talk. "Allergic to dogs? I don't believe it. It's the same as being allergic to air. Dogs are totally natural and essential to a good life."

"Dogs aren't essential to life." She opened the passenger door for Max and waited for him to settle. He had to get in the last remark before she closed the door.

"I said dogs are essential for a *good* life. Plenty of folks are out there living sad lives without a canine companion."

She shut the door without answering and circled to the other side of the car. Nala slid into her seat and closed the door. It was eerily quiet in her neighborhood, not a peep from a dog or a meow from a cat. Only the silent older sedans parked in driveways indicated anyone lived there at all. A few neighbors had resorted to electric golf carts to cruise the neighborhood. All the same, she shouldn't have been conversing with her dog outside.

"Max, you know you're not supposed to speak outside."

"Yeah, I know, but it's dark and late. The worst people might think is you're getting good at throwing your voice. You could have your own Vegas act. I could be your dummy, although I hate the word. On the other hand, some of your little, old lady neighbors might be excited to think you have an actual love life when they hear my beautiful baritone."

Nala rolled her eyes. "Not only do I have a talking dog, I also happen to have one who thinks he's a comedian."

Chapter Two

A T THE RED light, Nala leaned across the car to unroll the passenger window for Max. He immediately stuck his head out the window. The evening chorus of assorted night bugs filled the car the farther they drove away from the city. The streetlights vanished as she moved away from the populated area with an occasional security light lighting up the rural areas. The purposes of such lights were to discourage home invasions, but she had to wonder if it worked.

Silhouettes of houses and barns crouched in the distance. A smart burglar wouldn't touch these dark areas. Who knows what might come running out of the shadows? Anything from a pack of farm dogs to an irate owner with a shotgun. How would someone know if there was anything worth stealing in the dark? The well-lit homes offered more opportunities as far as window shopping. "Not sure why people use security lights."

Max pulled in his head to comment. "Yeah, like you didn't turn on the porch light before we left."

"That's different. It helps me get into the house, which is my point. Burglars can use the light to their advantage if the owners aren't home."

"Maybe." He turned away from her and shoved his nose out into the open air for a few seconds, then pulled it back in. "Pew! Pigs."

"You're not so sweet smelling yourself."

"Ha!" His shoulders slumped a little as he dropped his snout. "Really? I smell bad? Why didn't you ever tell me? Think of the places I've been, and everyone must have been commenting on how horrible I smelled. I have an image to maintain, ya know."

The possibility of smelling like a dog disturbed Max? She hadn't meant to upset him, especially considering Karly thought he was the key to cracking the case of the pet rescuer harasser wide open. Once her canine got obsessed with something, he gnawed on it to the exclusion of everything else. Yeah, he was a bit like a bloodhound on a scent when it came to that.

"Max, you smell fine. I was only joking."

His head went up. "Okay then. I was only joking about pretending to agree with you about the burglars and the light thing."

Technically, he hadn't agreed with her. "How would the lights be beneficial besides finding the right key to drive into the lock?"

"Simple. Those who have the bucks to invest, probably have security systems with cameras."

Nala gave a small groan, not out of pain, but because once again her dog had thought of something she hadn't. It made her doubt her own intelligence. "You're right. Videos would be useful to identify a robber. Most would have no clue they were there. Only those television criminals are smart enough to spray paint a camera lens."

"Spray paint? How does that work?"

"Never mind." Despite Max lacking an opposable thumb, it didn't stop him from trying to use the microwave. A lingering odor must have convinced him there was something yummy still inside. At least it hadn't been an expensive microwave. "You were right about cameras."

"Aroo! Aroo!" He howled in triumph, which was currently his new thing. When he finished, he gave her an abashed look before adding, "Keeps neighbors and relatives from helping themselves."

"You're worse than my father when it comes to being cynical." She patted her pants pocket to feel for the familiar phone shape. Bingo! She found it. A little strategic wiggle allowed her to retrieve her cell. New cars had Bluetooth systems that interact with the owner's phone without even touching it. That would be nice, but she'd have to wait a while before that happened. Besides, that would mean abandoning Natalie, her well-loved, but somewhat problematic car.

Using her thumb, she opened her phone and spoke into it. "Call Karly."

Max glanced back at her, possibly figuring she was talking to him. "I'm telling your dad you're texting while driving."

"I'm not texting. When did you get to be such a tattler?" Her dad and Max had formed a bond that none of her former boyfriends had managed to achieve with her police captain father. Most were probably worried he'd run a background check on them, which he sometimes did. A few might have worried about a credit check, which he also did. If any relationship progressed past two dates, her father might take a drive by the suitor's residence, just to make sure he wasn't married or living with someone. He didn't do that much anymore. She stopped mentioning her dates, not there had been that many recently.

She put the phone on speaker and placed it on the minimal dash. At least if her dog was going to rat her out, Nala would be able to state she had her eyes on the road and her hands on the steering wheel.

The ringing stopped, and Karly answered. "Where are you?"

"In the middle of the boonies."

"For real." Exasperation colored her voice.

"State Road 28. I think. I don't remember turning off it."

"Good deal. You'll turn onto 200 South after Campbell's Ditch."

"Is it a real ditch? Does it have a sign?"

"I don't know. Be alert. Remember you're not driving through Carmel with all their illuminated street signs."

"Only certain areas have those signs. Is there a sign for a dog shelter or something?"

"No. Fiona wanted to keep things private, which explains why she's so far from the road. Let me think about what you'll pass. When you turn onto 200 South, there's a dairy farm. There are all these cute black and white cows in the fields."

"It's night. I imagine a valuable commodity like cows would be locked up tight by now. Even if they weren't, I doubt they'd glow in the dark."

"True. Max could smell them."

"If I'm driving by my pet's nose, we're both in trouble."

Max shot her a dirty look, which probably meant he'd bring up the subject later. People who thought cats were divas had never met Max.

"All right. There's some city people that moved in past the dairy."

Nala didn't feel the need to point out to Karly that they were both city people. She allowed her to continue without interruption. She dropped her speed and peered into the darkness for a ditch named Campbell and 200 South.

"They have their place lit up like a Christmas tree with perfectly placed spotlights to draw attention to their Grecian Revival mini-mansion. That would be hard to miss. It's like Vegas in the middle of Tipton without the casinos."

"Once I see this showy place, how far would I be from Fiona's place?"

"Maybe a half mile."

Someone yelled in the background. "Make that two!"

The thought of her peering into the dark for two miles caused a slight twinge, which could be the beginning of a headache. Her headlights caught a junction sign and she turned onto 200 South. "I hope you realize what a good friend I am coming all the way out here, especially since I have preschool tomorrow."

"How's that going?"

"You ever hear complaints about education graduates not being able to get jobs?"

"Not really, but go on."

"Well, it turns out none of them want my old job. I'm just doing my school a favor until they can find someone. Maybe I shouldn't have agreed to do it, but I did. My goal is to get this wrapped up as fast as I can, catch some Z's before I have to deal with the junior drama queens and kings. A few almost hyperventilate when another child looks at them."

"Dogs are easier. I'll stay on the phone just in case you get lost. Fiona's house doesn't have a number, just an oversized blue mailbox at the end of the drive that has a huge brick enclosure around it to keep drunk teenagers using it for batting practice."

That would make it much harder to tell if the mailbox was blue in the dark. "All right then."

Some disembodied mooing in the dark sent Max into a barking frenzy. "Okay. Passed the dairy."

"I heard."

There was a dim glow on the horizon that had her peering at her small dash clock. It couldn't be dawn yet. It better not be. The illuminated dial indicated it was only a little past two, which was a relief. Otherwise, she'd have to make a U-turn and head back home. It would be like one of those alien abductee stories where the person had unaccounted hours pass or a blind date where she still lost a chunk of her night but was agonizingly aware while it happened.

Natalie, her car, chugged up the small incline only to be greeted by a light show worthy of any Christmas lights spectacle. The brightness after the sudden darkness made her blink. "Snicker-doodles! You weren't kidding."

Karly's laughter came over the phone. "I can't get over that you're still cookie cursing. Didn't you start that when you were eleven or so?"

"Can't remember. My father suggested it after I got in trouble over a non-cookie curse word. Mom blamed it on dad and some of his police buddies who didn't always censor their language, especially when watching a Colts' football game. The cookie cursing is so ingrained, I can't stop."

"It's cute, although it makes me think you must have cursed a great deal as a pre-teen for it to become a habit. You're halfway to the turn-off."

Nala didn't remember if she cursed a great deal as a tween. What she did remember was both her parents attempting to mold her into the person they thought she should be. Her mother hoped she'd be at least fashionable and in the limelight while her father's goal was for her to follow him in the force. It was no wonder she started cookie cursing early. Truthfully, she would have liked to join the force, but she had the double whammy of disappointing her mother and possibly not being the over the top cop her father would expect her to be. Likely, she'd be average. Even though most of the world crowded the average category, no one wanted to be accused of mediocrity.

"Is there anything I should look for?"

"Fiona! Is there anything she should look for?"

Karly yelled into the phone, causing Nala to wince. It wasn't the first time her friend had almost deafened her. The mute button was not something she ever made use of.

There was chatter in the distance. "The Kleins got a new John Deer tractor mailbox."

"Now, that would be a rarity in the country."

"Just keep your eyes open."

Max's barking interrupted the conversation, and her dog lunged halfway out the window. Fortunately, she grabbed his collar before he got anywhere, swerved, and stalled out the car. Large glassy eyes attached to a roundish head with a shock of feathers supported by a long neck stared at them. There was a low, almost growling sound that had to come from the bird since her hand was holding her dog that remained silent. Some greenery moved as three more large birds joined the first. Max, instead of growling, eased his body back into the car.

"Nala, could you roll my window up and get out of here?"

A reasonably high chain link fence served as a barrier for the oversized birds. She rolled up the window, not knowing that much about the birds. Maybe they could get over the fence with the right motivation. Karly's voice sounded somewhere near the floorboard.

"What happened?"

Nala located the phone and asked, "Why didn't you mention the oversized birds?"

"Oh, the emus. That means you're close. Look for the blue mailbox on your left."

Her GPS would have been much more helpful than Karly's directions, but it they were almost there. She started Natalie and steered her back on the pavement and crept down the road until the headlights caught a small brick mailbox closure that would frustrate any drunken teen with a baseball bat.

"We're here." She made the left turn into the gravel driveway.

Karly's voice filled the small interior as she asked, "Is there any way the two of you can walk up the drive and Max could smell for strange smells?"

Her canine lowered his brows and shook his head.

"Not a good idea. It's dark. We might step on something. There's bound to be chiggers. When you get right down to it, how would Max know if something smelled strange since he has never been here before? We'll drive up to the house, where we can walk around. See you in a little bit." She listened for Karly's agreement before she hung up.

"Good call, boss. No way I was getting out of the car. Monster birds could be lurking in the shadows." Max gave an all over shiver. "Those creatures could be waiting for an unwary dog." He added, after a lengthy pause, "Or human."

"Those emus wouldn't hurt you." She wasn't totally sure about that. She had read about disenchanted ranchers turning loose emus that had formed packs in Texas that were none too friendly.

"I could smell their intentions. They weren't good."

"Enough about the birds. Let's go over what you need to do. Karly thinks you can talk to the other dogs."

He gave an audible sigh. "I'll try. I'm no dog psychic, and I'm betting most of them are no Einsteins, or they wouldn't have been in the pound in the first place."

"You were."

"Hey, I was a special case. If that unhappy witch hadn't put a spell on me because my former owner and her boyfriend didn't talk to her, I would probably still be there sleeping on the couch, eating leftover pizza."

It almost sounded like he missed it. "You'd have lost out on all the great crime solving that you do now."

"True. Also, I do expect a cheeseburger since my ten-hour beauty sleep was cut short." He made sure to fix his liquid brown eyes into his best pitiful puppy expression. Despite the dimness of the interior, there was still enough ambient light from the dashboard to catch the shine of his eyes.

"Oh, all right, but you might have to wait. I imagine there will be few restaurants open as we drive home. Those that are will be serving breakfast, not cheeseburgers."

Max managed a put-upon sigh. "I guess I can make do with that colossal omelet biscuit sandwich they're always advertising on television."

"Yeah, I imagine you would." She almost rolled her eyes, but knew if she did, her dog would comment on it. It puzzled her how a dog who had been rescued from death at the shelter could be such a diva. It may have something to do with her treating him like he was extraordinary, which he was. It may have been her mother cooking for her grand-dog, as she liked to refer to Max. Nala always felt it was a dig at her for not providing her with any grandchildren. Then there was her father who would play endlessly with Max. Part of the time, he'd instruct her pooch in police procedure and how to apprehend the bad guy. No wonder Max was spoiled.

Exterior lights were on, highlighting a concrete block wall and some roof lines peeking above the fence. The iron gate swung open, and both Karly and a middle-aged woman, who she assumed was Fiona, stood in the middle of the opening with their hands fisted on their hips and their feet in a wide stance. Their pose resembled a superhero duo. Perhaps they fought for homeless pets everywhere.

They motioned her in and stepped out of the way so she could drive through. The gate slammed behind her with an ominous clang as she entered the interior. It reminded her of the commercial for some prison show that featured security doors closing with heavy metallic thuds. Did the dogs feel like they were in prison?

Inside the concrete walls was an expansive area. The safety lights must have a wattage equivalent to the sun. She parked Natalie near Karly's car, swung her door open in preparation of emerging, but Max climbed over her, using her leg as a springboard as he launched himself. He put his head down and went on sniff patrol as Nala exited the car, much slower.

Barking sounded in the distance, not frantic, just the occasional woof or yip, which was to be expected when a person had several dogs.

Karly met her and gave her a big hug. "I really appreciate your coming. You'll see why this is the perfect case for you and Max."

Case? She didn't remember anything about a case. Just that Karly needed a favor. She returned the hug, and then they both dropped their arms and stepped back. "Anything for my bestie."

"Ha! That's not how you sounded on the phone."

"Yeah, I know. You happened to interrupt a very good dream. It was as close as I have been to a date in I don't know when."

Her friend shot her an apologetic look. "Sorry. Maybe you can continue it later."

"I wish."

The woman dressed in black sweats liberally covered with dog hair strolled closer and held out her hand, ending any conversation of an intimate nature.

"Hi. I'm Fiona as you probably guessed. So glad you could come and bring your crime-solving dog."

Nala shook the woman's hand without mentioning she *was* the crime-solving element of the team. Make that her, and her obnoxious techie, Elvin, and her business neighbor, Harry, who had helped her in the past on surveillance.

"Nala Bonne, private investigator." There was no real reason to tack on the last part since surely Karly had already informed her, but she liked the sound of the title. It certainly was better than substitute preschool teacher. Even when she was the regular teacher, people seldom took her seriously, assuming anyone could do her job. After all, how hard could it be to sing alphabet songs and finger paint? It was much harder than she ever thought possible, considering the indulged darlings she had and their equally clueless parents who thought it unfair to put restrictions on their progenies. The only limits she wanted to put on the munchkins had to do with respecting her and the other students, which few did.

"Good to meet you. Karly insisted I call the police, which I did, but I'm sure the officer who responded filed me under crazy dog lady. I see your dog is already on the case. Why don't you have a look around and see if you can unearth some clues about the scum who'd dare torch my kennel?"

She gave the woman a nod. Yet another one who thought she'd pick up a vital piece of evidence, such as a driver's license the culprit conveniently dropped, and the crime would be solved. Nala gestured to all the lights that could have been easily seen by a plane looking for an airport landing strip.

"You had all these lights on and a person still approached your kennel?"

"Good heavens, no. I turn out the lights at ten to signal it's time for the dogs to go to bed. The morning sun awakens them. If I left these lights on all night, they'd never get any sleep."

Max lifted his head and glanced back at her. The slight angle of his head telegraphed his disbelief. Yeah, she never had a problem with Max sleeping with the lights on or in the middle of the day for that matter. "All right, when were you alerted that there was a fire?"

"A little after midnight when the perimeter alarms went off. Karly and I immediately turned on the lights. I grabbed an extinguisher and ran outside. There was a small fire next to the kennel."

"Not the wall?"

"No, the kennel, which means whoever it was had scaled the wall. I knew I should have put barbed wire or at least spikes on the top, but I didn't want the dogs to feel like they were in a concentration camp."

No one casually hiked all this way from the road, scaled a wall onto private property, in the dark, in a county where people were known to carry firearms. It appeared way too much work for a lark. "It looks intentional."

"Told the cop the same." She shook her head, and pressed her lips together in a mulish line. "Such a man."

"What do you mean?" The way she pronounced *man* with a sneer in her voice made it sound like more of a curse.

Her shoulders went up in a shrug as she explained. "Men tend to put women in categories. Such as hot babe, friend, mother, clueless old bag. If they're related to them, they might be more respectful."

"I don't believe all men are like that." She searched for an example that didn't include her father. "Harry, my business neighbor, isn't like that. He's very helpful."

Karly snorted. "You're so deluded. He's only helping because he thinks it will make you like him."

"I do like him. He's a great friend and occasional co-worker."

Both Fiona and Karly managed to say 'friend,' in unison.

Fiona grumbled more to herself than to them. "How can I expect hot babes such as yourselves to understand the trials of being an aging woman in today's world?"

Hot babe. That was a good one. "Your age shouldn't matter. You should still be treated with respect. You said you've received threats before?"

"Yeah. There was a note on my car. Phone calls to my landline. I dismissed the phone calls as a teenage prank."

Karly grimaced and added, "She doesn't have an answering machine."

It would have been nice to have an audio record of the calls. No one ever thanked you for pointing out the obvious, especially when they could do nothing about it. Fiona wagged her index finger as she spoke.

"I'm sure the cop thought the calls never happened."

"I doubt the cop thought that."

"Right, at least he took the note as evidence. Karly took a photo of it before the cop bagged it."

"Without a chain of evidence, there's little the police can legally do. That's where I come in. I'm going to connect the various elements into a strong chain. I have a recorder. I'm going to record our conversation. Is that okay?"

"I expected as much. Do you want to go in?"

Nala nodded, glad to leave the well-lit yard.

"Let me introduce Max to my dogs."

Karly came up on her left side. "Be prepared to be impressed."

Nala followed Fiona to the kennel, which had a keypad entry. She expected a clean kennel with individual dog runs, but when the door swung open, the colored lights cast a subdued light on curious dogs scattered around on couches and overstuffed chairs. One was even staring at a late-night talk show. Fiona gestured to the pooch.

"King Phillip is a bit of an insomniac. I've told him more than once the other dogs don't appreciate his television watching after ten, but he still does it."

Max padded in behind them and verbalized Nala's thought. "He can turn on the television?"

Fiona glanced back to see who spoke. Nala coughed and pointed to herself. "These allergies play havoc with my voice."

"I know what you mean. King Phillip can turn on the TV, but he can't change the channels."

"Good to know," Max conceded and managed to catch Nala's eye and wink.

For a moment, her pup was probably worried that there was a dog out there that could do more than him. The only way he turned on the television was by lying on the remote.

Fiona and Karly had stooped to pet a few heads and rub a few bellies, much to the dogs' delight.

Max used his snout to gesture to the door. "You go do what you need to do. I've got this."

Fiona gave Max her first smile of the evening, not demonstrating the least surprise that the dog spoke. "Karly let slip that you could talk to people. You certainly have an authoritative manner." She turned to Nala and added. "It must be nice having a dog who can speak English."

Nala raised her eyebrows in Karly's direction as she spoke through tight lips. "It has its moments."

Chapter Three

INSIDE THE HOUSE, two laptops sat close to one another on the kitchen table. They were surrounded by empty coffee cups, paper wads, and yellow legal pads with writing on them. A half dozen ink pens were scattered across the table while a small whiteboard leaned against a stack of phone books with the title GET FIXED PROJECT in bold black letters.

Nala gestured to the phone books. "I didn't know people even used those anymore."

"They have their uses," Fiona conceded, "with the least being that they're heavy enough to support things. Sometimes I can even get potential donor names from them."

The prospect of cold calling anyone did not appeal to Nala. How Fiona or Karly did it, even though it was for a worthy cause, was beyond her. Too many times, someone had called her about new windows, siding, or lawn treatment. She tried to get off the phone as soon as she could without being rude. Once, she'd even told a window representative that her water had broken and she needed to get the hospital. It wasn't one of her proudest moments.

"Do you call these people?"

Fiona pulled out a kitchen chair and straddled it. Her forearms went across the back of the chair and her chin rested on her arms. Instead of answering Nala, the woman addressed her friend. "Karly, I thought you told me your friend was smart. Here she thinks we can get people on board by calling them?"

Repeated by someone else did make her idea sound stupid. Her friend shot her an apologetic smile as she explained. "Nope. Calls would never work, especially since everyone has caller ID. Most would never pick up."

Although she hated to ask, Nala did anyhow. "Direct mail?"

Fiona snorted but mumbled something about straight to the circular file. Pleas for money tended to end up in Nala's recycling bin after she'd torn off her address. If none of these things worked, why were they up past midnight brainstorming about it? Feeling like she'd give it one last try, she suggested, "Email?"

"If only." Karly directed a grin her way. "It would make our lives much easier. Nope. We must show up in person. It works better if we have some adorable animal with us."

It was possible most people weren't all that thrilled about being trapped in their place of business or home while being asked for money. "Do you have lists?"

Fiona lifted her gaze and fixed a piercing stare on Nala. "Why do you want to know?"

The woman reminded her of Pamela Marcos, the grown-up version. Little Pammy had punched her out in fifth grade when she commented on her dress, saying she liked the color. Some mean girls had made fun of her before Nala's remark made her think it was more of the same, and she'd had enough. It had been hard to convince Nala's mother not to press charges. Most people would think it would be her policeman father who'd want to press charges, but her mother was more worried about her nose and had already contemplated the cost of plastic surgery. Her nose, however, survived the impulsive punch. Later, she discovered Pammy was a decent person. Maybe Fiona was, too. After all, she liked dogs. Her present mood could be lack of sleep, combined with dealing with some idiot who thought it was fun harassing women.

"The lists of who you visit might help us discover who doesn't like pets at all. Could be he didn't like being cornered in his home or business and made to feel guilty. It's probably someone who's totally passive and feels overwhelmed at telling you he's not interested in your cause. Could be he hates dogs, possibly frightened by a canine as a child. Does that sound like anyone you know?"

Fiona and Karly locked eyes as Nala contemplated how easy she could wrap up the case. She'd have a talk with the culprit. Charges would be pressed. Some jail time would be served, but no prison due to the overcrowding of the present system. She laced her fingers together and stretched them over her head thinking how much she could charge for a bare minimum of work.

Fiona gave her another dismissive snort and addressed Karly as if Nala wasn't standing less than a yard away. "You tell her. She's your friend. Ask her if she's going to take fingerprints."

Not the fingerprints again. Why did people expect her to always take prints? Television, murder mystery dinners, and video games tended to feature convenient, clear, full prints that could be easily identified. There would never be any other fingerprints nearby, either, to confuse the issue.

Nala angled her body toward Karly. If the woman wasn't going to talk to her directly, there was no reason to stare at her. Probably wouldn't do her any good to explain that prints were only good if a person had some on a database somewhere. Most didn't.

"Nala." Her friend caught her eye and made some motion with her chin in Fiona's direction that made no sense at all.

"Yes?"

"We haven't gone around to anyone's business yet. We are just in the planning stages of our campaign, which means whoever it is can't have been irritated by a cold call."

Not what she wanted to hear. She took a deep breath before pivoting back to face Fiona. "That means it's personal. Who have you ticked off recently?" *Besides me*, she added mentally.

The woman pressed a splayed hand against her chest. "Me? I avoid people as much as possible. Any idiot would know you must have contact with people for them to dislike you."

There might be a special exception for Fiona. No wonder the woman had turned to dogs for companionship. Still, it was hard to believe the woman had no regular contact with anyone. "Job?"

"I work from home."

She almost hated to ask, but she needed to know. "What is it you do?"

Fiona lifted her head and straightened into an erect seated posture. "I write cheesy greeting cards. It's all love and butterflies type of nonsense." She moved her right hand back and forth in a shooing motion. "You know, a total gag fest about how you're the best thing to happen to me type of stuff. It's the same cards men rush into the drug store to buy ten minutes before they pull into the driveway. They've forgotten it's Valentine's Day or their anniversary until some alarm on social media reminds them. That's the kind of crap I do every day."

That sounded unlikely, considering she had to be the most unsentimental person she'd ever met. Karly slid into view and gave her a quick nod. Nala had never thought about where greeting card sentiments came from, but now that she knew, she'd probably buy fewer cards.

"You're a freelancer? No boss?"

"None."

"Married? Divorced? In a relationship?"

"No to all three."

"No surprise." Had she said that out loud? Karly's horrified expression told the story, but Fiona laughed.

"I value someone who speaks her mind. That's why I like dogs. If they're hungry, they'll tell you. If they don't want to be bothered, they might give a little growl or a snap to make their point."

Fudge. Why hadn't she'd seen it before? Fiona spent so much time around her dogs, she had no clue how people acted. That made things a little bit more understandable. "All right, no relationships ever?"

"Seriously?"

Nala kept her face expressionless and gave a short nod. "You'd be surprised how long some people will wait to pay back a grudge."

The woman gave a sigh, pushed off from the chair, and started pacing around the kitchen table. "There was a boy who I had a thing with when I was in art school."

"How long ago was that?"

"About thirty years. I can't remember. It was my junior or sophomore year."

"His name?" Nala knew she was going through the motions because some fling from thirty years ago could hardly matter now, but her father had cautioned her to turn over every rock, dismiss nothing.

The woman managed a wistful smile, shocking Nala. "Jack, his name was Jack."

Nala pulled out the notepad she decided to carry for such information. It made it easier than having to listen through an entire recording and she could add impressions she got that wouldn't be on the tape. She did both to be thorough and set out the recorder as well. She patted down her pockets for a pen she'd placed there. No luck. She snagged one from the table as Fiona went into another pace around the kitchen.

"Okay. Did Jack have a last name?"

The question stopped the pacing. Fiona held one finger up to her lips as her eyes rolled upward. "Jack. Jack Dubois, Dewitt, Dewier. Oh, I'm not sure. It's been so long ago. I find it hard to believe someone I knew when I was twenty would come looking for me now, especially to harass me."

Nala wrote the possible names and put a question mark beside them. "I agree, but I need to be thorough since you have no clue. Do you have a suspicion? Maybe emu guy resents having dogs close to his expensive birds."

"Duh. He has no clue. I brought the dogs in under the cover of night. Before I even built the kennel, I played a tape of barking dogs and backed away from it to see how far I had to be before I couldn't hear them. You can't hear them until you're well on your way up my drive, such as it is. There's no way anyone knows I even have dogs."

"Someone does, or I wouldn't be here. Who comes up that drive on a regular basis?"

Fiona glanced at Karly as if she'd provide an answer. Her friend waved. "There's me, of course." Then she pursed her lips. "The delivery guy."

"Yeah," Fiona agreed. "I order everything online. Their food. The treats. Even their medicine."

"I imagine that person must have a clue you have dogs."

"True but the delivery man told me what a great service I was performing. In fact, he told me he had two rescue dogs himself. I don't always get the same delivery person, though."

A delivery fellow didn't offer much motive, but so far that's all she had besides some dude named Jack that Fiona could barely remember. Sounds like it must have been just one of those things as opposed to the love of her life.

"Did the other delivery man act strange?"

"No. It was a woman. She asked me for details to start up a cat sanctuary since she loves cats. I couldn't give her a whole lot of details, except that it might be easier than a dog shelter. Cats tend to enjoy staying inside and are quieter."

That was no help. It didn't necessarily mean people meant what they said. It could have been a ruse to put her at ease. "Did you believe the delivery people?"

"It didn't matter much what I thought about them. Gus trusted them." Fiona folded her arms as if the subject had been tabled.

"Gus?" Maybe there was someone else living here.

Hearing his name brought an elderly beagle slowly wandering into the kitchen. Each careful step hinted at arthritis. Fiona knelt beside the dog and hugged him. Her voice morphed into a low, soothing tone as she reassured the old hound.

"I'm so sorry we woke you, Gus. Would you like a snack since you're up?"

The dog managed a lazy tail wag in response. If the dog thought the delivery people were okay, she knew there was no way she could argue the point with Fiona. What she could do was ask Elvin, who had a way of hacking into computers to get the names of regular drivers. She might then be able to pull the criminal records on them. Speaking of dogs, she should check on hers.

"I need to check on Max."

Fiona scampered off the floor where she'd been putting dog treats into the beagle's mouth. "I'm sure your partner has the case sewn up by now."

She wished. Otherwise, the favor might turn out to be a time suck with her chasing vague leads that weren't useful. The three of them turned in the direction of the back door with Fiona swinging it open. Max sat smack outside the door.

How had her dog left the kennel? Second thought, she wasn't surprised he did. Despite his four legs and a snout, he often considered himself slightly above the average dog. "How did you get out?"

"Otis, the boxer, let me out. I swear those boxers can use their paws like hands. I'd like him to teach me how to do that. It would be ever so much nicer than waiting for you to open doors."

Fiona chuckled and patted Max on the head. "I'm sure he would, but maybe you could teach a few of my dogs to talk in return."

Nala found herself shaking her head. Max kept her busy and at times annoyed with his constant quips. It would be hard to imagine what twenty plus dogs would be like. Max's verbal ability was due to a witch spell gone wrong, which made her doubt dogs could be taught to talk.

Fiona must have considered the idea for a moment or two longer because she grimaced. "Never mind. If all my pups were talking every minute of the day it would be just like being surrounded by people. They'd lose their dog appeal. Forget I asked."

Just as well since there was no way that Max could make it happen. "What did you find out?"

Even though she asked, she expected a big zero. After all, she was the sleuth in the group, although Max had helped, especially in chasing away the creepier elements. Most of his observations were ordinary, except when it came to smells. He had that area cornered.

"Could I get some water? My throat's a little dry."

Fiona rushed off to get crime-solving dog extraordinaire some water. She returned with a stainless-steel pet dish and a bottle. "I hope beef flavored water is okay."

Beef flavored water? Nala had never heard of such a thing.

Max barked and then added, "Yippee!" He finished by giving Nala a significant look.

She knew he'd ask in the car why she'd been withholding beef flavored water. It probably cost the moon, and quite frankly, water should not taste like meat, in her opinion.

Gus stood on unsteady legs as Max noisily lapped up the water. The beagle made a determined but unsteady line to the bowl, then pushed his head closer. Max immediately sat and allowed the older dog to finish the water. Sometimes, Max's compassion surprised her.

He glanced up at Nala. "You might want to get the name of that water. Tasty."

Fiona handed her the empty bottle. Nala turned it over to see an image of a happy dog and lettering she knew wasn't English. *Nope.* Max would have to settle for plain old water as opposed to something she couldn't pronounce or afford.

The shepherd cleared his throat. "Officer Max, ready to report."

"Proceed." She hadn't told him to call himself Officer Max. It sounded like something her father would do.

Max cleared his throat again.

Fiona hurried over to the cabinet and retrieved another bottle of water. "Do you need another drink?"

"No," Nala answered for him. "Go ahead, *Officer Max.* Give us your report." She instinctively knew he wanted to be addressed as *officer.* Was it a telepathic message or the result of living with the opinionated dog? It could be a little of both.

"First off, I have a few messages for Fiona. Penny doesn't like the lamb and rice dog food you switched her to. King Phillip wants you to know there is nothing good on television after ten. I suggested the classic movie channel. Soldier would like to move to the house if King Phillip is going to watch television all night. Agnes wants you to know she's the one who ate the potted plant by the grill. She's sorry, and it wasn't as yummy as she thought it would be. Not the least bit like hamburger."

Fiona nodded her head. "I thought as much."

Max continued. "Lancelot would like a firmer bed. As a legendary warrior, he doesn't like the super soft cushion."

Really? With his ability to talk all he got was a laundry list of demands from the pampered rescues. Nala gave a small huff of frustration. "Did you get any information from the dogs about the intruder who set the fire?"

"They were asleep until the alarms woke them."

"What about King Phillip?"

Max tilted his head one way, then another. "He was watching a WWII movie, and he thought he heard a thump and someone curse in German, but that could have been the movie."

Could King Phillip understand German or did he just make it up to impress Max and the other dogs? "Anything else?"

"Twinkle Toes insisted it was a man, an alien, or possibly a unicorn. Whatever it was, it had male energy."

Seriously, this was supposed to be useful? Fiona nodded as if accepting the peculiar statement as fact.

"Twinkle Toes does have advanced psychic abilities. Karly told me her former owner ran a fortune telling shop on Broadway."

No need to mention that would be the same as equating Max with the ability to teach preschoolers since he lived with her. "So…" she drew out the word hoping Max would catch her intonation as she spoke. "Anything else?"

"Yes. Bloody the bloodhound smelt the lingering odor of cigarette smoke."

"He could detect it with the smell of the fire?"

"Please. He's a bloodhound. A regular turbo nose when it comes to sniffing out things. We might want to take samples for Elvin."

"Yes, you're right." Too bad her dog had thought of this before her. Often with arson, whatever accelerant was used to start the fire could serve as a calling card. Max still had his snout up at an awkward angle, letting her know he was waiting. *What a diva.* "Thank you, Officer Max."

"You're welcome." He managed to say the words through his upward pointing snout and then dropped to a normal level.

"All righty then, I think Max and I should head out after bagging some samples." No reason to mention her second job since that would make her sound a bit incompetent if she needed two jobs to stay financially afloat.

Fiona passed a gourmet dog treat to Nala. "I know he can't eat on the job, but you can give it to him later."

"I will," she promised.

Max, Karly, and Nala exited the house and maneuvered around the kennel to the scorched area where the fire had been. The outside lights provided enough light, but Nala still clicked on her flashlight. It was part of her private eye kit she assembled, along with baggies for samples, cellophane tape, and baby powder for fingerprints.

A few squeezes on the powder bottle liberally coated the top of the wall close to the spot on the ground where the fire had been set. "I suspect he hopped the wall here but may have come over somewhere else. If the gates were open he could have waltzed right through them, but that would be ridiculous considering Fiona has made the place as secure as Fort Knox."

"Not exactly."

The hesitant tone in her friend's voice had Nala looking away from the powder dusted bricks. "What do you mean?"

Karly looked over her shoulder, searching for anyone who might be listening. Finding no one, she still moved a little closer.

"I have the code for the gate, which I used to get in. They swung closed behind me, but I didn't check to see if the lock had engaged. Fiona had made a point of mentioning to me that the lock wasn't working right. I didn't check. Figured I'd be leaving in a couple of hours, and I could check then."

"So," Nala drew out the word, imagining the scene when the alarms went off and the two women ran out of the building, "did you push it shut when you came out to investigate?"

Her friend kicked at the ground and hung her head. She admitted in a whisper. "I saw the gate standing open about a foot. I got there before Fiona and slammed it shut."

"Why did you do that?"

Karly's thin shoulders went up in a shrug. "Don't know. Maybe guilt. Fiona and I have become friends since she adopted all the dogs. I would go so far as to say I'm probably the only person she likes."

"I can believe that. It also means I'm wasting my time looking for little oily spots in the powder where fingerprints might be."

"You can try the gate."

"I will. Probably won't get anything due to your fingerprints, or there are no prints on record, or our potential arsonist was smart enough to wear gloves."

"Don't you hate a smart criminal?"

"You have no idea. I'll get the samples and be on my way before Fiona grills up a steak for Max."

The dark ashy residue crumbled as she attempted to put it into the baggie. An errant breeze blew most of it away. The familiar acrid smell of burnt paper started the sleuth cogs rumbling. Paper burned fast. It didn't sustain a flame. It wouldn't be enough to sustain a decent fire, especially considering the rains they had recently. Maybe the fire wasn't the threat Fiona thought it was. Maybe it was a distraction. She'd just have to figure out the motivation, which should be a snap with no real suspects and a spotty evidence trail.

Who was she kidding?

Chapter Four

THE DASHBOARD CLOCK read 3:50, not quite dawn, but close enough. By the time Nala got back home it would be closer to five, which would leave her a grand total of thirty minutes for a nap since she needed to be at school by seven. The children didn't arrive until 8:15, but she had to check her email for unexpected meetings, fire drills, or parent notes informing her that one of the little darlings had lice or strep. Usually, it turned out to be the same one she had been hovering close to for shoe tying purposes.

She had to lay out the materials for the day, which often involved cutting and copying. If she had come in on Sunday to do it, she wouldn't be as rushed, but she wanted one lousy day off with no responsibilities. Most of Sunday was spent at her parents' house lounging by the pool as her mother detailed their upcoming cruise. Her father had been off somewhere training Max, possibly insisting he should answer to *Officer Max*, which would explain his recent behavior.

"If only I had some free time. Even an hour or two would be heaven." She gave a heavy sigh that caused Max to pull in his head from his usual pastime of feeling the wind on his tongue and sniffing the air for possible fast food aromas.

"What's up?"

"No time."

"Do you mean no time to get my cheeseburger?" His ears went

up as if alarmed.

The people who thought men had a one-track mind had never met her dog. She'd place him against any male. If they made cheeseburger dogfood, she'd buy it. However, no one would since it didn't sound healthy. Instead, her pup would have to make do with lamb, brown rice, and yam kibble. "I told you it's too early."

"IHOP is open." His face morphed into hopeful expectancy with the words.

"How do you know about IHOP?"

"Elvin."

"Should I ask?"

"Remember when your parents were out of town for some reunion?"

"Yeah." She and Karly had decided to do part of a wine tour and booked a room at a hotel that didn't accept large dogs. Small yappy dogs were fine, but not large ones, which made no sense to her pooch. Elvin had surprisingly volunteered to watch him. Nala had never asked why because she thought it might be better not to know what her often outrageous, sometime business partner did that weekend. Since her dog didn't come back with any piercings, complaints, or tattoos, she figured everything was fine. "Go on."

"Elvin wanted to work on my detective skills."

"Did you talk to him?"

"Not him. I was pretending to be a regular dog."

"Almost afraid to ask." Nala flew down the backroads, praying no wayward cow would be standing in the road or a lurking deer would be waiting in the shadows for a motorist to pass by. A little speed in the wee hours of the morning shouldn't hurt anyone. No one was up yet, not even the chickens.

"Elvin had this harness that made me look like a guide dog."

"Of course he did."

Max continued, undeterred at the interruption. "Anyhow, he thought he'd get in the act and don some dark glasses and pretend to be blind. Our first stop was IHOP where he got me the cheeseburger platter."

Nala groaned. With Elvin getting him a combo plate, her father sneaking tidbits off his plate, and Harry keeping jerky treats in his office just for Max, it made sense why her dog often turned up his nose at normal pet food.

"That was the extent of your playacting? Didn't anyone wonder about a blind man driving away?"

"We parked in the next lot, so the folks from the restaurant wouldn't see him. Then we went to the local watering hole."

"He took you to a bar!"

"No. Elvin called it a watering hole. There were lots of video games and people around your parents' age."

"Oh, that place. That's not too bad then. They let you in?"

"They had to because I was a service dog."

"A fake one." Nala turned on her brights since there was no one around to blind. It might save the life of any raccoon or possum she'd have to swerve to miss.

"It was all part of the act. Things were going well. Elvin had ordered me some sliders, bite-size burgers."

"I know what they are."

"At least you got to eat yours. I only got to smell them before Elvin was kicked out of the bar."

She had to ask but knew she'd regret it. "What happened?"

"Elvin was being the blind dude. A woman was sitting at the bar. Elvin said something about feeling her since he was blind. Turns out the bartender, her husband, didn't like the suggestion. Came around the bar, all red-faced and cursing, muttering about how he didn't care if he was blind and assisted him to the door. I felt compelled to go with him, leaving my sliders behind."

"A great sacrifice."

"A huge one."

"Why did you never tell me?"

"Elvin swore me to secrecy until the twelfth of never. Figured that must have been last month or so."

"Yeah, around there." People joked about dogs not being able to tell time. Apparently, they didn't do archaic expressions, either. She had no clue how long the twelfth of never was, but she assumed it was a very long time.

Max managed to smirk in the dim dash light. It wouldn't be too unusual for her pooch to try to stir up trouble between her and Elvin. She gave her dog another considered look when she spotted something white out of the corner of her eye.

Her right foot hit the brake, a second before her left foot hit the clutch. In the process, her hand must have found the horn, but not intentionally. Her car fishtailed a little on the gravel, then came to a shuddering stop.

"You better deal with the runner you almost killed."

She almost ran over someone. That had to be a joke, right?

A voice sounded outside the car.

"Hey! Hey you! Got something against runners?"

Here she thought Max was playing her. The memory of the spot of white returned. It had seemed odd against the backdrop of the night-shrouded trees. A man-shaped silhouette climbed out of the ditch and approached her car. Yep, he was wearing a white T-shirt. *Oh, lemon bars!*

The only decent thing would be to apologize. She rolled down her window as the man approached, limping a little. His leg might be hurt, but it had no impact on his yelling voice as he strode to the car.

"What were you thinking driving like a bat out of hell down a dark country road?"

Something tugged at her memory as the runner came closer. Could be her intuition was warning her to get out of there pronto. Wasn't this how most of the ghost stories started? A lone person driving down a desolate country road when a person approaches and asks for a ride. *No rides.* All rides were out of the question, not like she was going to offer one.

The headlights exposed his bare legs and minuscule running shorts. His white T-shirt stretched tight against his chest. If he had a weapon, she wasn't sure where he would hide it. She should say something. Although she couldn't think of anything appropriate for the occasion.

"Sorry. Didn't expect anyone on the road at this time of the night."

"Morning," he corrected and came closer to the car. Max, who had been monitoring the man's progress, gave a friendly woof.

The angry tone morphed into surprise. "No, it can't be. Nala? Max?"

Hearing his name, Max gave two more hearty barks. Talk about horrible luck. What was the possibility she'd almost run over Tyler Goodnight, the handsome cop her father had tried to fix her up with? She hadn't minded the attempt, but it had spiraled out of control and into crazy town with her last case. Everything became too twisted to explain, and Tyler faded away, never bothering to call her again.

"Um, Tyler?" Her hand went up to her hair she'd twisted into a messy bun as she zoomed out of the house on her way to Fiona's. Her plans, if she ever ran into Tyler again, did not involve stained sweatpants or a faded T-shirt. Nope, she'd planned to be bedecked in her best black dress hanging on the arm of a prime piece of male eye candy.

The only male she had beside her was the canine kind. Her turn-coat dog was happy to see the man. Tyler bent to peer into her car.

"Hello, Max." He made eye contact with her. "Nala."

Snickerdoodles. Despite tousled hair and a sweat-soaked T-shirt, the man still reeked of sex appeal. "I wasn't trying to run you off the road."

"Could have fooled me." His lips kicked up in a lazy smile that set loose the butterflies that must have been sleeping in her stomach. That he could have such an effect on her was so not right. Last time she'd seen him, he had thought the worst of her. Imagined there was something between her and Elvin, her prankster friend, who wasn't above stirring the pot if given half a chance.

Why did her body have to go all gooey at the sight of him? "What are you doing out in Tipton?"

He straightened up and stepped back from the car. "Staying with a friend. You?"

Her mind seized onto the word *friend.* Every female knew that was code for *woman.* If it were a man, Tyler would have mentioned him by name. "Case."

"Should have known. Could you give me a ride back since I may have strained a muscle when I jumped out of the way of a certain out of control driver?"

"I was not out of control." She gave a slight exhale, wishing she'd seen him before he dived for the side of the road. "I guess I can. Max, get in the back."

The shepherd mix carefully stepped over the console to the backseat.

Tyler opened the passenger door and slid into the recently vacated seat. He closed the door and gestured to the road. "Keep going down another two miles. I need to get showered, dressed, and on the road since I'm working today. It's a long drive."

"Don't I know it."

If he wanted to save time, he should get a girlfriend closer to the city. She drove in relative silence, thinking how bold it was to get one woman to drive you to a different chick's house.

Tyler filled up the passenger seat with his long legs and wide shoulders. Even the smell of his shampoo and sweat sucked all the breathable air out of the car. Every breath she took was pure Tyler. Why did she agree to this?

"You still seeing that Elvis guy?"

"It's Elvin. Not Elvis. I was never seeing him, but you never gave me a chance to explain." She snapped out the words, angry at the physical effect he had on her.

"Oh, really?" A suspiciously happy tone colored his words.

"Why should you care? I'm driving you to your girlfriend's house. I bet she won't be too thrilled to see me in her driveway."

"Up there. The John Deere Tractor mailbox."

"Which one?"

"The third one."

She turned into a driveway crowded with a pickup truck, a car, and a bass boat on a trailer. "Well, you're here. See ya."

Whatever she lacked in friendliness, Max interjected his own affability by placing his snout on Tyler's shoulder and gave him a thorough swipe with his tongue.

"At least someone still loves me."

Nala didn't even fight the eye roll. The man was so full of himself. Unfortunately, he had reason to be. The front door slammed. *Gingersnaps*, an awkward scene she didn't have time for. A bearded man strolled into sight and placed a tackle box and rod inside the truck.

"Hey, what's this? You met a woman while jogging at the butt crack of dawn. This is so unfair. I live here. Any single women around here I should get first dibs on."

Tyler swung the door open. "No biggie. Just an old friend from the city. After she ran me off the road, she felt obliged to drive me back."

"I did not run you off the road. You chose to jump into that ditch."

Laughing, the man in the fishing vest came over to her side of the car and put out his hand. "I want to shake the hand of the woman who put this cocky SOB in a ditch."

Nala rolled down her window and shook the man's hand. "Nala Bonne."

"Oh, you're that one." He waggled his eyebrows and grinned.

Tyler groaned and gave the man a slight push. "C'mon, man. Don't go there."

Had the military veteran turned cop given her a second thought after he decided not to phone her? "What one is that?"

A well-aimed elbow from his friend had the bearded man coughing. "Never mind. Name's Wayne Peterson. Local boy. Single. If you want to know more, I tend to spill all when plied with liquor and food."

"Wayne, stop it." Tyler pushed his friend away from Nala's car window. "Ignore him. Been nice seeing you. Don't want to make you late to wherever you have to be."

She held up her hand. No one had to tell her twice when she wasn't wanted. "See ya." Max added a bark to their goodbye. Instead of reversing down the long driveway, she made a torturous turn that consisted of endless minute moves under the eyes of both men to get her car angled down the drive. Fortunately, neither one felt the need to yell out instructions, although their thoughts were broadcasted by their folded arms and amused expressions.

She missed the gene that allowed her to reverse down long drives fast. That didn't make her inferior to those who could. Natalie, her car, bumped onto the road, allowing her to escape. Her eyes automatically went to the dashboard clock that showed it was twenty minutes later than the last time she looked.

"Look at the time! I'm so behind schedule."

Max chose to climb over the gearshift to the front seat, but one paw slipped on the gearshift. The gears ground, forcing Nala to step on the clutch before her antiquated transmission gave out. The smooth transition she expected ended up in a jerk, then a stall. *Fig bars!* Maybe she should consider her mother's idea of leasing a nondescript car for business purposes. At least it could be an automatic. The charm of a stick had worn thin, especially in heavy traffic or when stopped on a hill.

The hefty check she received for her last case disappeared fast when she decided to pay the rent for her office in full for a year. At the time, it sounded like the smart thing to do considering she wouldn't have to worry about having a continual load of cases. There were also the tools she bought, although Elvin insisted on calling them toys, such as the parabolic microphone, night vision goggles, and a digital camera. On the fashion side, she bought herself an Indiglow watch and expensive trench coat with a matching fedora. So far, she'd only worn the entire ensemble once. It made her more obvious than allowing her to blend in. Indianapolis wasn't London. A few people did wear trench coats, but even fewer wore them with a fedora.

The growl of an approaching engine reminded her that she was stopped in the middle of the road. It might be a rural road, but with morning coming, it would be filled with those who had a job in the city. She turned to Max who had his head out the window as usual. "Okay, bud, we need to leave before that car gets here."

A SUV slid past her with a honk. Rude, even if she was somewhat blocking the road. *Wait.* Hadn't she once seen that same navy SUV in her family's driveway or at least one like it? She shook her head and sighed. It probably wasn't Tyler. All she had to do was see the man once, and he totally took over her thoughts. Whoever it was had vanished around the bend in the road. If it was Tyler, what did the honk mean? The usual meaning would be to get out of the way. However, people who knew each other would honk at one another as a friendly gesture.

Her hand slapped the steering wheel in frustration. "I don't have time for this."

"You really don't," Max added, "Especially when you need to stop and get me a treat for what an excellent job I did."

The car engine chugged to life as Nala decided against answering Max's claim. He really had come up with more evidence than she had at this point. The case might distract her away from the unresolved feelings she had whenever Tyler Goodnight was mentioned. Case, focus. She maneuvered the car down the roads being alert to possible runners or navy SUVs, of which there were zero.

What did she know so far? Fiona had received vague threats she felt were directed more at having a personal dog kennel than at her. All she knew was someone started the fire, possibly spoke German, and smoked. It wasn't enough to run a check on anyone. Normally, she'd assume it was someone close, such as an ex or a neighbor. Hadn't had much luck on that angle, but something might turn up.

Sometimes crimes happened when someone wanted attention. This was probably what the officer who took the complaint thought, Karly was the one who insisted on calling the police, realizing there needed to be a documented chain of events before things escalated, working on the assumption they would.

Still, she pondered the idea as she drove closer to the city. Stepping on someone's property where the owner could welcome you with a blast from a shotgun appeared bold. A fire pumped up the audacity of the individual. It would be easy enough to label Fiona the culprit and call it a night. Three things wrong with that theory. Fiona had no great love of people, didn't want their attention, and was inside with Karly when the fire started.

How legal was her impromptu shelter? Maybe the area wasn't zoned for shelters or multiple dogs. She'd have to consider that. Her father would know.

"You just passed IHOP," Max announced with a certain amount of alarm and a slight whine at the end of his voice.

"Yeah, sorry about that."

The idea of standing in line for about forever to get her dog a treat did not appeal. Still, maybe she could get something, too. At least that would save some time. She checked both ways before making a U-turn on the empty street and drove in the direction of the brightly lit restaurant. It amazed her that Max could even recognize it. However, when it came to food, her dog was a champion at recognizing food signs, although it could have been the scent.

A few cars were scattered around the restaurant parking lot, but not enough to indicate busy. Some had to be employee cars. She'd parked close to the door when she noticed a navy SUV. No, it couldn't be. Other people could drive SUVs, and some of them could be navy, and one of those other people could have decided to go out for breakfast.

As she debated what to do, Max poked her arm with his snout. "Come on. You're the one who is constantly harping about time."

Yeah, she was. He had a point. She reached under her seat for her purse. *Nothing.* That couldn't be right. A slight rush of panic went through her veins as she twisted in her seat to feel in the back seat. Nothing except for her detective bag. Had she'd even brought her purse? "Max, have you seen my purse?"

"The bag that holds poop bags and sometimes dog treats?"

"Yes."

"I did."

"Where?"

"At home, on the hook by the back door."

She groaned. In her rush, she must have grabbed just her phone and detective bag, which was a little more than an old laptop bag with cellophane tape, baggies, notepad, pens, and baby powder. She kept adding more stuff as she thought of something. Maybe her dog was wrong. Perhaps she'd left the purse at Fiona's. She could call Karly and ask. Not that leaving her purse behind at Fiona's would make it any better, but at least she would know where it was.

Her hands smoothed down her pants, feeling for a tell-tale phone bulge. Oh, no, where is that phone? On top of that, Max gave a few excited barks. She knew the tone. He recognized someone.

Slowly, she turned her eyes to her right and saw Tyler walking out of the restaurant with a to-go sack and a cup. *Lemon bars!* With any luck, he wouldn't notice Max barking his head off in pure joy.

The man turned and walked toward their car. When he was close, he bent to look into the window.

"So, we meet again?"

"Ironic, huh?"

"I'd almost say you were following me."

That was the last thing she needed. For him to mistake the two of them being in the same place as her trailing him. It would be a minor leap for him to assume she was obsessed and stalking him.

She forced a laugh. "We stopped to get Max a cheeseburger. He's kind of a cheeseburger nut."

"I can identify." He rattled his sack near the window. "At this time of the morning, this was the only place I could get a juicy burger."

She'd almost swear the man was teasing Max by rattling the bag and sending the smell into the car. Sharp nails bit into her leg as her dog made a lunge for the bag through the open window. He snagged it with a quick snap and backed, wiggling into the back seat.

"Max!" She twisted in her seat to grab the sack back. "Give me that."

The German shepherd mix used his body as a shield as he huddled over the bag and ripped through the paper. It would only take him seconds to inhale the food. It wasn't like she could buy Tyler another burger since she'd left her purse at home. At least she hoped it was at home and the phone was in her detective bag.

Time to face the music. She turned back to Tyler who had the cup in front of his face, but she could tell by the crinkles at the side of his eyes that he was amused as opposed to being angry.

"I'm so sorry. I guess he really wanted a cheeseburger."

"I see." He held out his right hand and flexed it. "Well, at least there's no teeth marks. I kinda deserved it. Max probably thought I was offering it to him."

She wasn't so sure about that, but maybe her dog still had a touch of the street dog in him, from when he had to live by his wits before being picked up by the dog catcher. Not knowing what to do, she smiled up at Tyler.

"Why don't you let me replace that burger? It's the least I can do."

He grinned and angled his head toward Max. "I might have to do a better job of guarding my burger next time."

Tyler's phone chimed the same time she remembered she'd forgotten her purse. How could she take back her offer without revealing she was driving around without a license?

He glanced up after reading his text and shook his head. "I'm going to have to take a rain check on the burger. Got to go in earlier than I thought. Maybe," his eyes took on an interested gleam, "you could buy me the burger later. I would even pop for yours. It would give us a chance to catch up."

The unexpected text saved her from revealing her license-less state, but now she was in a quandary. Her first instinct was to say yes, but he was the one who wrote her off before. He jumped to conclusions at Elvin's inferences that they were involved. He had never asked her or at least that is what she assumed happened. From the back seat, Max answered, "Yes, Tyler, I'd love to."

Max ignored the dark look Nala shot her interfering canine, before she looked back to the man in question who laughed.

"That's great! Love the dog ventriloquist act. You're certainly unique. I'll call you later to see how your schedule is shaping up."

Tyler straightened up, held up a hand in parting, and flashed that wicked smile that made her insides into a gooey soft center.

"See ya." She started up the car as Max jumped into the front seat and licked his lips.

"Good burger. You can thank me later for what I just did."

Chapter Five

THE MORNING SKY pinked up from the sun's rays reaching up from the horizon, which only reminded Nala of all the sleep she had missed. Instead of snoozing, she was headed home without her phone, which would make it hard to call Karly to double check on her purse. This is what happened when you woke someone in the middle of the night. Right now, she should be in her bed with only seconds existing before her alarm went off. The possibility of still being asleep was a pleasant one. Realistically, Max would have woken her by now.

"What do we know about the case?"

She talked out loud to reason things out. Nala heard even Einstein did that, so it must be a time-honored method of solving conundrums. Often, her dog would pipe in, convinced she was talking to him. Every now and then, he had some good intel.

"We know you didn't get paid," Max chimed in, failing to realize he wasn't included in the conversation.

That was true. A woman who had money to build a state-of-the-art luxury kennel should have a few bucks to discover who was threatening her precious hounds. "It was a consultation. It's like getting an estimate."

Max gave her a long look before continuing. "Did you talk about money while I was in the kennel?"

They hadn't. Her dog, who was normally concerned with food

and the occasional squirrel, was starting to sound a great deal like her father. Maybe he was being coached by her parent. "Did Dad tell you to say that?"

Max looked straight ahead, which was always a tell when lying. "It doesn't matter what the Captain said to me. Did you seal the deal?"

That *was* so her father's statement. "No, I didn't, but I will."

"Elvin doesn't work for free."

How did her father manage to insert all his pithy comments into her dog? It might not be that hard. Max loved to mimic people, which could be tiresome since she often left the television on when she was gone to entertain her pooch and confuse the neighbors if Max started talking to himself. For one whole week, he walked around saying, "Luke, I'm your father," in that low creepy Darth Vader voice, which he pretty much nailed.

"No, he doesn't. I'll contact Karly. Surely Fiona would pay my daily wage if she cares so much about her dogs."

"They have orthopedic mattresses, by the way." He somehow managed a wistful wheedle.

Really? He was going there? The whole thing about what a great life those dogs had compared to his. "I'm willing to bet your mattress is much more expensive than their beds."

"Where is this luxury mattress?"

"It's my bed. You sleep on it every night."

"Oh, yeah. I forgot."

"That you did. Also, I doubt those dogs get cheeseburgers when-ever they nag."

Max cocked his head as if considering the possibility. "The ones in the kennel get a high-grade kibble, but the old one in the house gets whatever he wants."

"Sounds like someone I know."

Bark! Bark! Bark! Bark!

Max didn't laugh as well as he thought he did. It ended up sounding like barking, which confused her. Every now and then, he would do *ha ha* but usually in a sarcastic manner. That she blamed on Elvin, who often would use the derisive *ha ha* when she made a joke he didn't find humorous or when she poked fun at him.

"Doesn't matter if you agree with me or not. Here's the deal. Once we get home I have to get ready for school in a flash. I'll let you out in the yard, and you better take care of your business because I will not be pleased with any surprises."

Max looked away and mumbled, "One time I had an accident, and you never forget."

It was more than once, but she decided not to mention it. Too many other things to concentrate on besides getting ready for school. She had to contact Elvin to run the test on what she was sure was paper doused with lighter fluid. Her father could get her information on how many dogs a person could own. He might even give some insight on the unhelpful officer. She didn't want to mention his name since this could all be a wild goose chase. Karly may have befriended someone with a couple of screws loose. Even the mentally unbalanced could have good traits, such as being an animal lover.

The traffic picked up as those on the first shift headed to work. Fortunately, the exit to her neighborhood was only a few blocks away. Nala slowed and braked to make the turn. She held up her hand in greeting as she slowed, expecting a more verbal greeting from the trio of walking elderly women on the walk. The women, bundled up as if it were January as opposed to the end of September, gave her a long look in unison.

The one sporting a red hat gave her a censorious stare. What had she ever done to her? She must have heard about Max chasing grandchildren. Her more opinionated neighbor, Viola, she recognized by the feather on her hat. She wasn't sure if Viola was a bird lover or frustrated hunter, whichever led her to festoon herself with feathers.

Viola cupped hands around her mouth and yelled, "Who's the lucky man?"

The question so startled Nala, she hit the brakes. It explained the other look she received. Determined to straighten the women out, she leaned in Max's direction to talk out the open window.

"I had some work to do."

The three women, instead of talking to her, turned to each other.

"That's what they're calling it now?"

"I rather believe her. Look at her, she's a mess, and she took her dog, for Pete's sake."

"Goodness, the poor thing needs help. Don't you have a nephew that's single?"

Somehow, hearing someone else talk about her love life made it sound infinitely worse than it was. "Enjoy your walk, ladies."

She put the car in gear and drove home in a funk. Max, never great at interpreting moods, decided to rehash the women's remarks. "You are a mess."

"Watch it, buster. You could end up sleeping outside."

He swung around with an open mouth. "No way! I was only repeating what your neighbors said. It would be hard for me to determine if people looked good or bad to each other. I do know whatever you look like, your cop friend was still interested."

"Yeah, he was. Weird." The house loomed ahead, and she bumped into the driveway, parked, switched off the engine, and jumped out in less than a minute. Max followed her out her door, probably afraid he'd be forgotten in the rush.

"Remember, backyard."

Instead of answering, which he seldom did in clear sight of the neighbors, he managed a sullen expression.

Before Max, she would have sworn dogs had only three expressions, happy, guilty, and I'm going to rip your face off. Her dog not only had more emotion than any other dog, he also managed to pack in the drama. Maybe she should stop letting him watch the soaps.

Inside the house, she started the coffee and let Max out before she hit the shower. As she soaped up her hair, she pondered the impromptu invite Tyler had issued. Something about her buying him a burger. Since saving a client messed up their previous date, she'd have to make sure nothing canceled this one. Who knows? It might be the start of something. Did she want to start anything?

Sometimes. Other times, no. Relationships should be simple, but they so seldom were. There was a cartoon where aliens watched single humans go on dates, then drive home alone. The aliens concluded they had nothing to worry about since humans couldn't even mate successfully. The film was probably made by some bitter, divorced person, which didn't make it any less true.

The problem with going out with Tyler was she might like him, which wasn't a horrible outcome, but it could turn out he didn't like her once he really got to know her. Then there was the issue if things did work out, they could become a couple. He might keep a uniform at her place if he slept over, and she wasn't sure she could handle someone else in her house. Would she have to start stocking up on beer? Would she have to hide all her feminine hygiene products so he wouldn't be freaked out by them like Jeff was? No wonder she was single.

It had been months since she'd been on a date, never mind a relationship. No one ever called her a party girl or serial dater. After her relationship went bust with her former boyfriend, she didn't trust her judgment on men. Before Jeff announced that he was moving on to someone else, she assumed everything was okay and that they'd eventually marry. It took her a long time to get over that, not the relationship or even Jeff, but the fact that she could be so deluded.

It wasn't like men never asked her out or her friends never tried to fix her up. They did. Nala shot down anyone before they even had a chance. She imagined scenarios that could happen from one random snippet of information. With her imagination, she should be writing science fiction.

Part of her knew this would be as close to a date as she would get. It wasn't like she'd be dating any of her students' parents. That would be a little on the icky side, especially considering how open the children were about sharing information. She didn't want it spread around that she made home visits, which she didn't. If she did, on hearing that, a few of her pint-sized students would have meltdowns as she hadn't visited their house yet. Besides, most of the fathers were married, and the few that weren't, Nala totally understood why their wives had left them. The bigger mystery was how they convinced a woman to marry them in the first place.

The private eye business didn't bode well for romantic prospects, either. So far, only women had hired her. Even if a man did hire her, getting involved while on a case would just confuse things and be unethical. Despite Karly's belief that Harry had a crush on her, she knew better. The man could use the cash. That's why he helped her out.

By the time she got out of the shower, dried her hair, and

dressed for pre-school in eye-popping primary colors, she'd decided to go out with Tyler. The open back door allowed Max to saunter in at will, which he did. He wandered over to his empty bowl and slammed it with his paw.

"Quit being so demanding. I'll get you some food." She suited her actions to her words and poured some kibble into his bowl. He sniffed the expensive no-grain dog food and walked away. He acted like it would kill him to eat it in front of her, but the bowl would mysteriously empty itself while she was gone.

Weren't pets supposed to give unconditional love? Maybe that was all bogus? People assumed a great deal from their pets that couldn't talk. If they knew their pampered pet's true feelings, Karly might find more than a few extra animals at her shelter. On the other hand, if people couldn't talk and people merely attached whatever feelings they wanted to the other person, then relation- ships would probably work better.

A knock sounded on her door, stopping her philosophical wool- gathering. "Who could that be?"

"You could answer the door and find out," Max remarked and angled his head in the direction of the door.

"Aren't you supposed to be barking your head off and terrifying whoever is on the other side?"

"My bad. Woof. Woof. Howl."

She rolled her eyes as she walked to the door and opened it to Karly's grinning face. Her friend held up Nala's phone.

"Thank goodness you brought that by before I left for work." She reached for the phone.

Karly raised an eyebrow in Max's direction. "Woof, Woof?"

"Not my best work, but I knew it was you."

Karly wrinkled her nose, not entirely buying Max's excuse.

"Yeah, of course." She sniffed the air. "Do I smell coffee?"

"You know you do. It's in the kitchen. Help yourself. It's the least I can do since you gave me the only useful device I have in maintaining some semblance of order in the classroom. Just the sight of my cell phone instills fear into some of the little darlings' hearts. They're afraid I might call mom or dad."

"What about the ones who aren't afraid?"

"I videotape them and send the video to my father in case I go missing."

"Be serious."

"I am being serious." She only joked about forwarding the videos to her parent.

Karly went into the kitchen and poured herself a cup of coffee. Nala got one for herself. "You really didn't have to rush here to return my phone."

Karly shrugged as she hunted through the kitchen cabinets in search of sugar. "I needed to get back. I have to see Fiona's lawyer this morning."

"Why is that? Is she putting you in her will since you're the only person she can trust to take care of her precious pups?"

"Yippee!" Karly held aloft two small packages of restaurant sugar she'd located in the junk drawer. "You're right about I'm the only person she can trust. She wants me to have power of attorney if anything should happen to her."

"It was a paper fire. Nothing life-threatening. Every Fourth of July my parents end up with bottle rockets in their pool, but they don't assume someone has it out for them." Even though her words made sense, she didn't entirely believe them. Fiona lived in the boonies with no close neighbors. The phone calls were easy enough to make, but traipsing through the brush at night took more effort.

"Yeah, I agree. It wasn't the fire that mattered, but the intent. Someone wants to scare her."

"I agree. The question is why."

"Fiona thinks the hatred is directed at the dogs."

"Could be. They're a motley crew, but not a vicious dog in the bunch. Some of them are so old I wonder if they have any teeth left to bite anyone."

"True. We're going to do the legal paperwork and then see if we can't get some short circuit televisions set up around the property. You know of anyone who does that type of thing?"

"I'll ask Elvin. I was going to call him anyhow."

Max bumped into her leg. Nala glanced down at the dog who was moving his mouth, but no sound was coming out. "What?"

"I was trying to be subtle. Ask her about being paid."

How could she have forgotten about that? "I was wondering…"

Before she could continue Karly held up one hand. "Wait. I have your retainer. Fiona wrote you a check after you left. Said something about she didn't know if you were worth it, but Max certainly was."

Max pranced around the kitchen with his nose elevated. Nala chose to ignore his theatrics.

"How do you know what my usual retainer is?" It was weird since she hadn't officially set one yet. So far, she'd been charging a hundred and twenty a day plus expenses. Her father had informed her that was way too low. After some investigative work of other small-time firms, she found they usually charged a hundred and fifty a day, even if the work was a routine background check that took less than an hour. Nala hoped to grab some business by undercutting them.

Karly smirked. "I had no clue, but our family lawyer insists on a retainer of sixteen hundred before he even considers doing anything."

"What if it is less than sixteen hundred?"

"Trust me. Nothing is ever less than sixteen hundred." Karly pulled a white envelope out of her bag and handed it to Nala. "You'll be able to pay Elvin. Tell him to put some speed on it, too. I know you probably think the woman is looney tunes, but I happen to know she's scared. Why else would she want to give me power of attorney?"

"You're a trustworthy person who loves dogs. Sounds like a perfect fit to me."

A peek at the check wouldn't hurt just to make sure Karly hadn't misunderstood. Fiona hadn't struck her as overly generous, except when it came to dogs. There it was in bold script, a sixteen followed by two zeroes. Heaven. She pressed the check to her chest as she considered some of the things she could use it for. Maybe she would buy Max a bottle of beef flavored water since he was the deciding factor on even getting paid. She tucked the envelope into her bag with the intention of depositing it in the bank if time allowed. She might even do it if time didn't allow. That way she wouldn't have to worry about possibly losing it.

More than once she'd caught one of her students in her purse. Recently, despite locking her purse in the file cabinet, Logan, one of her more out of control students, used safety scissors to break into the cabinet. Apparently, the boy didn't differentiate her purse from his mother's. His excuse was that he wanted candy. When informed, his parents acted pleased at his problem-solving skills as opposed to being appropriately horrified.

After gulping her coffee, Karly placed the mug in the sink before replying. "I agree, I'm a super cool person."

"That's not what I said."

"It's the fact that Fiona wants to give someone power of attorney. As far as I know, people only do that when someone is mentally incompetent, gravely ill, serving in a war, or frightened something might happen to them."

This was all true. "People also get a power of attorney when they're afraid someone else in the family might file for one. This usually happens when money is involved. The grasping relative usually mentions a few odd incidents. Little things, such as carrying on conversations with deceased individuals or wandering the neighborhood in their pajamas, that may or may not be fabricated, but enough to make a judge think the person who is asking means to help the poor, incompetent soul. The threat of that happening usually inspires the person in question to get his or her own legal warrior."

"What?" Her friend blinked twice. "You're not making sense. I'm no warrior, legal or otherwise. You already know Fiona has no husband, no real ex, and no children."

"Siblings?"

"None. If she had to portion out her inheritance, she probably wouldn't have been able to build her cast-off pups their luxury condo."

"Money is always a prime motivation. Maybe she named someone in her will who might want to inherit a little faster."

"No, absolutely not!" Karly shook her head vigorously side to side.

"How would you know? People have killed for money." A quick glance at the kitchen clock reminded her she had no time for debate. What she needed to do was find something for lunch and hope someone was generous enough to bring in bagels or donuts for breakfast. It might be a futile wish, but it was all she had since nothing edible that could be eaten while driving existed in her fridge. A frozen stuffed pepper entrée would work for lunch, but only if she let it thaw in her room since none of her colleagues would be understanding of anything that took ten minutes to cook in the microwave. It would barely leave her time enough to eat it.

"Yeah. I've read the papers and have seen the news magazines. Still, all the same, I can personally guarantee that this is not the case this time."

Nala snagged her lunch bag that she'd picked up from lost and found last year after no one had claimed it for a month. A few other teachers had had their eyes on the bag, but mostly for their children. She should have felt somewhat ridiculous toting a bag with mice dressed as princesses, but it was a very nice insulated bag. "How can you guarantee anything?"

"I happened to know she's leaving whatever money she has left to the shelter."

"Yeah, I should have thought of that. What about her home and dogs?"

"Ah, yeah, that." Karly cleared her throat. "That's held in trust for as long as the dogs live. The trustee administers the estate and receives a stipend. At the death of the last dog, the estate can be sold, and the money from the sale will go to the shelter."

"That means all her money is literally going to the dogs."

Max wandered through the kitchen. "Good one. I would have said that if I'd been paying attention."

To know she and her dog were starting to think alike was no great honor. It even alarmed her a little. She held up her index finger. "Am I right in thinking you are *that* trustee?"

Karly nodded and sighed.

"No one thought it may have been a conflict of interest to give you power of attorney?"

Her shoulders went up in a shrug. "Dunno. I guess we'll find out later this morning. I suspect you pay a lawyer, and he does whatever you want him to."

Nala added a soft drink to her lunch. The caffeine should keep her from falling asleep in the classroom. Fear of what the students might do should serve to keep her alert. She could wake up to find her hair decorated with paper clips and her fingernails colored with permanent markers, which would possibly extend to her hands and clothes, leaving her to serve as a cautionary tale to other teachers to promote a good night's sleep.

"Well, lemme know. It could make a significant difference."

"What do you mean?"

Karly was the sister she never had, but as much as she loved her, she knew the woman's idiosyncrasies. She tended to freak out over possibilities. "Oh, it's nothing really since I'm fairly sure this is all a childish prank."

"And? Don't think I don't know when you're hiding something from me. Go on." Karly balled one hand on her hip and pursed her lips.

Her father once joked that when Karly had decided to wait something out, she had more tenacity than a snapping turtle, which was exactly what Nala didn't need right now.

Nala snagged her purse and headed for the door. "I should have left already."

"Yeah, you're in such a hurry you forgot your pretty princess lunch bag." She held the item out to Nala and squeezed past her to the porch. Karly's dog-mobile sat behind her bug, blocking her in. For a person who didn't own a dog, she had enough dog themed bumper stickers and car magnets on her minivan to earn the assumption that she was a crazy dog lady. She even had a bumper sticker announcing that. Karly followed her out onto the porch.

"C'mon! Just tell me. I will imagine the worst. You know how I am."

Before closing the door, she fixed Max with a stern look. "Be good."

Instead of responding with a yes or even a nod, he gave her a lazy smile that could result in unexpected surprises and not the good kind.

"Keep in mind, I'm not totally sold on Fiona being in danger, but let's say she was, then I will assume the motivation is money. That would make you as future trustee and person with power of attorney as the next target."

"Thanks a lot. I could have done without knowing that."

"You asked."

"Yeah, I did, but you could have lied."

Chapter Six

THE SECRET TO not being noticed was to blend in. People, in general, saw what they expected to see. If he didn't look too different, he wouldn't arouse any suspicions. Toby pulled at the business polo that chafed his neck. He wasn't sure what type of material it was made from, but rubbing against his skin it felt like insulation, the fiberglass kind. It probably wasn't the material, but the disguise he'd donned of khakis and a company shirt with a local water distributor embroidered on the left pocket with a blue raindrop dripping from it. The designer who penned it possibly thought it was cute or whimsical. Toby didn't do cute.

His time in prison sucked out all of the whimsical, too. The two things that kept him going was retrieving the emeralds that had inadvertently sent him to prison and paying back his partner who'd hung him out to dry. The key to both was in their old office. Gabe, who Toby hated to admit was the brains of their partnership, came up with the idea of renting an office like a legit company. He even made up a business card about *No Job Too Small* without saying what they did.

Their phone number was on a burner cell they switched every so often. This also resulted in not buying too many business cards at once. They never bought cards at the same Staples, either. Gabe thought a curious employee would think it odd that they kept changing the number on their business card. Toby thought no one would notice, but he trusted Gabe in the matter since he used to run a legitimate business. Toby's expertise included circumventing security systems and safes. Both were getting so sophisticated he needed to up his skills, which he did by getting a job with a security system company that paid the rent on his tiny studio apartment for the past few months. It certainly was better than darting into the YMCA, pretending to be a guest of a member, just for a quick shower.

He rubbed his hand over his head feeling the bald spot his new haircut revealed. His employer, Justin, a young guy, insisted that people felt better if those installing the systems didn't resemble felons or drug addicts. Instead of fussing about it, Toby stopped at a barber for a conservative cut and shave. There was only so much scrutiny he could take, even though he'd already laid out a couple hundred for a fake ID and social security number.

He even managed to convince Justin, who was divorced, to dole out his paycheck in cash to avoid his ex-wife taking everything he got. It was a good plan since he had no clue if whoever's social security number he had was living or dead. The living tended to watch the credit scores, while using a dead man's number could cause issues, too.

A man turned the corner and headed for the building with the ground eating strides that signaled both energy and being on the right side of thirty. Ah yes, the pigeon, and he was right on time. Since Toby had been studying the building for almost a year, he knew who came and went. Harry, punctual like clockwork, was his best chance. He always arrived at seven and left around five or at least he had for the entire month Toby had cased the place.

Toby strode from the shadows making sure not to make any noise until Harry was on the steps and fumbling with his keys to get in.

"Hey! Could you hold the door? I'm here to pick up the empty water bottles."

Harry half-turned and nodded. "Sure, man." He glanced at Toby, then asked. "No new bottles?"

Damn, a smart one. He hated those. "No. The customer decided to stop service. Thought it was too expensive. Boss still wants me to get the empties because those things aren't free." Mentally, he congratulated himself on his quick response.

"Yeah, I wouldn't know. I make do with tap water." He smiled, shrugged his shoulders, and held the door open.

Toby acknowledged his gesture with mumbled thanks and moved past him to reach the stairs. He couldn't move faster than Harry because he'd see where he was going. His foot lingered on the first step, stalling.

"The empties are in the basement. I saw them when I went down there yesterday to look for boxes."

"Ah, yeah." He gently knocked the heel of his hand against his forehead. "I don't know what I was thinking."

Toby turned to go downstairs. He'd have to take the bottles with him and abandon them in an alley. The lower he went the staler the air smelled. The light switch was where he remembered.

A flick of the lights illuminated a room with abandoned metal desks and worn roller chairs pushed into a corner. New primary colored bins labeled glass, paper, and aluminum looked out of place with all the dust-covered mementos of days gone by. An oversized sign announced a clearance sale and a roll of carpet with a bent corner revealed a geometric design in blues hues. It reminded him of the one Gabe had in their office. He thought it made the place look hip and trendy.

Toby kneeled to examine the rug closer. It was the one that had been in the office. His heart skipped a beat. He'd assumed Gabe either took everything or what was left had been tossed. This opened all sorts of possibilities.

Maybe Gabe really did get in a fatal car wreck. Toby assumed that was a cover just in case the authorities connected the two of them. The real question was not if there was an actual wreck, but where the emeralds ended up. It didn't take too much work to discover the insurance case was still open. Rich people were like that. It didn't matter how much money they had. They still were very protective of their stuff. No way would the case be closed until the gems were found.

The gleam and weight of the emeralds flashed back into his mind. He didn't just grab the various jewelry cases crowded into the safe. Instead, he opened them with his latex glove-clad hands, making sure he was getting the requested item. The ornate setting was heavy with expensive stones and had an elaborate, almost lattice setting that looked old.

He'd bet the lady of the house wouldn't be caught wearing something so dated, but that didn't stop her from wanting it back. His art skills might not be top notch, but they were good enough to sketch out an image of the gems to show Henri, a jewel thief, who managed to successfully elude capture. He hadn't seen them or heard about anyone trying to fence them.

Since all the leftover furniture was moved to the basement, maybe the answers were here. Thanks to the ever-helpful Harry, he might just find the information he needed without taking the risk of breaking into the third-floor office the chick and her dog took over. It depended on if he could find the jewels or any information leading to Gabe.

Once, he'd overheard her and Harry talking about investigating someone. A private eye taking over their office was a laugh. He wasn't too worried about the woman, but the dog was another matter. He swore sometimes when he was hiding in the shadows, watching the comings and goings of the building's occupants, that the big black dog would stare in his direction as if he knew Toby was there.

WITH NO DONUTS in the lounge, not even a donut hole, breakfast ended up being a granola bar Nala scrounged from the back of her desk drawer. She couldn't remember ever buying that brand. Maybe it was something left over from the daily snacks the parents provided. At least she hoped so as opposed to being left there by some former teacher eons ago. Maybe granola bars were up there with Twinkies as far as never decomposing.

Lunch allowed her a quickie phone call to Elvin who agreed to meet her at the nearby Paneras. He mentioned Hotel Tango that was earning itself a name as a trendy bar, but she wanted to discuss business and that involved being able to hear.

After she dropped her tiny possibility grenade on Karly this morning, her friend had texted her six times. Once to let her know she did get the power of attorney. The other times included messages about a black Cadillac that she was sure was owned by the Mafia, following her too close. Also, there was a person who stared at her at a red light. The list went on. Good thing she had it on vibrate since they weren't supposed to use their cells during classes. This was why Nala hadn't wanted to say anything about danger to Karly in the first place. If she hadn't been tired and sleep deprived, she would have resisted, not only for Karly's peace of mind, but for her data plan, too. At this rate, she'd run out of minutes before the end of the month.

The day couldn't end soon enough. Right before she put the last child on the bus, her middle-aged principal notified her that a parent was waiting to talk with her. *Gingersnaps!* There was a rule about them making appointments as opposed to just dropping in. Since the principal was only months from retiring, he tried to avoid conflict as much as possible, which often meant avoiding the parents. On the other hand, he wanted the teachers to handle any issues, so he could make the smooth cruise to retirement where the only kids he'd interact with would be grandchildren.

Her last pint-sized student hugged her, wiping the hand he'd used to pick his nose on her sweater. *Yuk.* No time to wipe off her sweater. The best she could hope for was a lack of snot. Nala ran through her room, turning off lights and closing windows. She had no intention of coming back to the room before leaving. She left her door open since everyone knew a closed door meant you didn't want the janitorial staff to clean. Preschool classrooms should be hosed down and disinfected daily, but a quick vacuum was what she usually received.

In the conference room, Lyndsay's father crossed and uncrossed his legs. A nervous reaction that felt wrong. Even though they had only met twice, she considered him a practical person. Lyndsay was never one of her problem children. Lately, she had noticed, however, the child's elaborate hair bows were missing and her hair, instead of being in complicated braids or curls, was simply brushed.

Nala entered the conference room door and threw a brief smile in the father's direction while she glanced around for any support staff. No teachers. No counselor. Not a single administrator in sight. If possible, a teacher gathered witnesses to avoid one of those *he said she said* types of conversation. With some advance warning, she could have bribed her fellow pre-school teacher, Brenda, to stay. Everyone else was making a mad dash to their cars as soon as the last student left. Their contracts stated they had to stay an extra thirty minutes after school hours, but no one enforced it. Instead the administrators competed with the teachers for the privilege of getting out of the parking lot first.

The school secretary and the afterschool care staff, along with the janitor, were probably the only employees still in the building. It wasn't as if she could call any of them in to witness. Maybe it would be something simple such as a whispered admission that Lyndsay picked up lice or learned an unsavory expression from another student.

Get it done and get out of there. She held out her hand to the father. "Hello, Mr. Norwood." He stood and grasped her hand in what she would call a non-shake since there was no pumping of the arm. It was similar to one of her male students who always tried to hold her hand whenever she wasn't holding anything.

This was getting awkward, especially when the man stared at her with pain-filled eyes.

"What can I do for you, Mr. Norwood? Lyndsay has no issues in class."

He finally released her hand and collapsed back into his chair. "I'm grateful that Lyndsay hasn't been acting out with everything that has been going on. That must be your influence. She idolizes you and wants to be just like you."

Nala gave a forced laugh, thinking the girl wanted to be a lackluster teacher who made up stuff as she went along since she was too determined to make her private eye agency into her real job. She sat and steepled her fingers in front of her face, wondering if she should have brought pen and paper. Of course she should have. How else would she remember anything?

"Is there anything I should know?"

The man sucked in his lips and glanced down at his hands before meeting Nala's gaze. "Bliss, my wife, left me. Called me at work and asked me to be home in time to meet Lyndsay's bus."

"That's awful!"

He propped his elbows on the table and cradled his head in his hands. "You have no idea what it's like being left to be a clown."

"Ah," she paused, not knowing what to say. "Leaving your family a note that you took off with another man is never good." Did she just say that? Talk about rubbing salt in the wound.

Mr. Norwood pulled his head from his hands and raised his eyebrows. "I said she left me to *be a* clown, not *for a* clown. She took off for clown school. It's always been her dream."

In the scheme of things that wasn't as bad as being left for another man. "Maybe she'll come back soon. How long can clown school take? Think of the upside. She'll be able to make balloon animals for Lyndsay's birthday parties."

"Yeah, I guess. I'm worried about my daughter. Maybe this is only for a couple of weeks, but I'm afraid the glamor of the circus could overwhelm my wife."

"I'll keep an eye on Lyndsay."

"I'd be grateful if you could give her some extra mothering. That would be nice, too."

That would be a challenge. She had never been a mother and was clueless what extra mothering would consist of. Did he want her to brush the girl's hair or make sure her socks matched? "I'm glad to help. I'm sure everything will work out." She stood as a cue that the meeting was at an end.

Mr. Norwood stood and held out his hand again for a final shake. Once again he engulfed her hand with his larger hand and made no effort to release it, making Nala a trifle anxious. Plenty of men, hurt by a wife or girlfriend, tended to label the entire gender worthless and struck out at the most convenient representative of the sex, which would be her. Her eyes went to the glass window in the door. No convenient person was peering inside, giving her an excuse to cut the awkward meeting short.

"Well, I need to go. I have to meet someone."

"Of course." He dropped her hand and sighed. "I'm sure a pretty, single woman like you is dashing off to meet some smitten guy. What's it like to be in love? I thought I knew, but now I'm not so sure."

Super awkward. "It's not a date. It's business. Still, I'm sure your wife loves you and your daughter very much." The last part she felt obliged to add since the man was so sad.

"Really?"

His eyes lit up at the possibility, which forced Nala to lie a little more. "Oh yes, I have no doubt." She moved one hand behind her back to cross her fingers just to cancel out any lightning strikes for lying. She forced her lips into a smile. "Bye now."

Protocol dictated she wait for the parent to leave the building before she was allowed to. Even her lie didn't energize the father to move faster. The skin on her face tightened as she held her fake expression, certain saying anything else would prolong the visit. His odd question if she'd ever been in love did make her wonder. Had she?

If someone asked her that a few years earlier, she'd have named the various celebrities she had crushes on as a teen, certain she was the perfect woman for any of them, if they could just wait for her to grow up. They didn't. For a while, she considered herself in love with Jeff until he left. A man in love just doesn't get up and leave his beloved, especially for another woman. That meant at least one of them wasn't in love. The immediate time after that, when she wasn't cursing the man's name, she wondered if she had ever loved him. Wasn't love supposed to heal everything? It hadn't made him stay, which made her think maybe it wasn't love.

What if it was love and love was not enough? Why was she holding onto some outdated belief that wasn't true? Women were told that love made everything better, keeping neglected wives in marriages that weren't working. It could all be a plot. Yes, that's what it was, a plot. Who started it? The government? The church? All those magazines about having a lovely home and garden? The same publications announced on their covers that you could drop thirty pounds in a month along with a recipe for a rich, chocolate cake.

"Bye now. Thanks for talking to me."

The words brought her out of her warm-up to an existential crisis about the nature of love fueled by too little sleep and self-doubt.

"Ah, yeah. No problem. Anytime."

Lyndsay's father arched his eyebrows. "Anytime? Really? I may take you up on that."

Nala squeezed her eyes shut, trying to turn off the glimmer of interest she saw in his eyes. It had to be a mistake. If not, then it totally explained why his wife would take off for clown school. Most women would have headed in the direction of a lawyer's office or a marital therapist.

The outside door closing served as a signal to open her eyes under the assumption the man had left. He was still there with a bemused expression on his face. It must have been someone else escaping to the outer world, leaving her stuck in this limbo.

"I was thinking," he spoke with a happier tone than before, "since I shared such intimate details with you, it's only fitting that you call me Michael."

"No need for first names, Mr. Norwood." If the man was looking for some flirtation she was so not it.

He placed one hand on the glass door and pushed it open.

Thank goodness, he was leaving. No reason to see him ever again, except when she had duty in the car drop off area. She'd just wave him on then. Maybe she wouldn't have to endure too much awkwardness since the principal might interview her replacement tomorrow.

Michael Norwood stepped into the doorway and glanced back over his shoulder. "Goodbye, Nala."

Brownies! How did the man know her first name? She certainly hadn't told him. She had, however, told her pre-school class, thinking that sharing a name with a movie character might be a bonding strategy. It also was easy enough to click on the school website and scroll down the staff names.

Even though she needed to be at the restaurant now, she waited a few extra minutes to be certain she wouldn't be stuck carrying on the awkward conversation in the parking lot.

Nala slipped into the empty principal's office to peek out the windows facing the parking lot. It was odd that he left his office unlocked as he bolted along with the rest of the staff.

Michael gave one last look at the school before climbing into a white SUV and driving away. Okay, it was safe to leave. She'd call Elvin from her car, so he'd know she'd be a few minutes late.

"What are you doing in my office?"

The irate voice startled her. Nala turned slowly, allowing her fingers to fall from the blinds as she grasped for a reasonable excuse. "Oh, I was waiting for you." An excellent stall technique she had to admit.

"Here I am. Why were you waiting for me?"

She inadvertently blew out a long breath, not quite prepared for the question, but while her father worked hard to teach her the letter of the law, her sometime babysitter Rhoda taught her how to skirt an uncomfortable situation. A lie presented with a kernel of truth always worked best.

"I wanted to know if you've hired anyone yet for my position."

The man placed his hands on the small of his back as if it hurt. "Not yet." His lips pulled down a bit. "You'd be surprised that despite all the recent elementary graduates not too many are interested in preschool."

Not exactly what she wanted to hear, but she could use the extra money. Most would have thought teachers avoided teens like a plague. News must have leaked out about the preschoolers unable to tie their shoes, wipes the noses, or inability to keep their hands off other students. As far as teaching went, it was double the work with none of the glory. An average teacher expected a student to be in control of his or her own body while a preschool teacher merely hoped.

It wasn't that she didn't like children or even teaching, but it would be so much easier with eight or ten fewer students. An assistant would be another nice touch, but reduced school funding cut the aides. Nala and the other teachers had to depend on volunteer help and room mothers. In today's economy, parent participation was practically non-existent. Most would show up for holiday parties, then bicker among themselves and be less than helpful, countermanding her instructions.

"Oh." It was hard to know what to say when she was torn between not wanting to teach and needing the money. "Anything? Anyone?"

The man gave a heavy sigh as if he was caught between a rock and a hard place. "School has already started everywhere. Those who wanted to teach are teaching."

She knew, also, that not everyone who had an education degree wanted to teach. "How about mid-term graduates?"

He slanted her an odd look. "Are you that unhappy here?"

A mental alarm sounded in her head. *Trick question, be careful how you answer.* Although her goal had been only to work a few months until they found someone, she had also counted on pulling down some more money cases. Even the hack work of investigating online dates hadn't turned out to be the cash cow she'd hoped it would be. Women in the Circle City must like the dash of danger in not knowing if their date was a single airline pilot or a sociopath with mother issues. A man could be both, which would be hard for her to pinpoint if he didn't have a police record.

"Certainly not. Got to run. Have a dinner engagement." She flashed him a forced smile and held up her hand in goodbye.

"See you tomorrow."

Nala gave a short nod and exited the building. What had he meant by see you tomorrow? Did he think she was so unhappy with her job she'd ditch work? Natalie, her red Beetle, looked abandoned in the middle of the parking lot. Earlier today, she'd managed to snag one of the last open spaces.

Safely inside the car, she started the engine and turned on the radio. Usually, Max was with her and offered his own running commentary that he interspersed with comments on any fast food establishment they passed, often with the hope she'd stop and get him something.

"I wish Max were here." She gave a sigh as she maneuvered the car out of the parking lot. "If he were, I'd tell him how lucky he is. As a dog, he wouldn't have to fake smile at all the various males in his life."

Thank goodness she was on her way to see Elvin. No need to waste any of her contrived smiles on him. More than likely the man would cause her to groan, wrinkle her nose, and occasionally laugh.

Chapter Seven

THE SCENT OF coffee competed with the smell of baking bread as Nala pushed open the door. Even though it wasn't quite dinner time and well past lunch, the agreed upon restaurant bustled with people. Many huddled over laptops while nursing a cup of coffee and nibbling on a sugary pastry. Most appeared to be young, teenagers or a little older. The free WiFi drew them or the lure of escaping from their parents' watchful eyes.

The center of the restaurant hosted the largest tables. A group of older women sporting flamboyant red hats sipped, nibbled, and occasionally burst into uncontrolled laughter. They must be enjoying themselves. Her gaze passed over them as she searched for Elvin. He certainly wasn't among the computer surfers. There were a few couples in the booths, instead of talking to each other they had their heads bowed over their phones as their fingers flew across the keyboard. She wondered for a second if they might possibly be texting each other. If they were, why did they even bother meeting in person?

Where could Elvin be? Oh, no, she forgot to send the text telling him she'd be late. He probably left. Another shriek of laughter had her turning back to the red hat ladies. Their big hats would brush one another as the women squirmed with merriment. One of the diners stood, revealing among the midst of solid women in pantsuits the tall, gangly form of Elvin.

He waved in Nala's direction. "Ah, look, my date has arrived."

Every one of the women turned to stare at her with some interest and a few felt free to comment.

"Oh, so she is."

"She's a cutie, just like you said."

One of the women waved vigorously at her. Not knowing what to do, Nala took a step forward. "Hello."

The waving woman stood up and hugged her, wrapping her in a cloud of perfume. She whispered in Nala's ear. "I'm so glad to see Elvin with a decent woman. Thank you. Please, please, give him a chance."

After giving Nala an extra squeeze, the woman stepped back, allowing Elvin to introduce her.

He grinned and gestured to the woman. "Looks like you met my Aunt Mabel and charmed her from a distance."

"Pleased to meet you."

He motioned to the other women. "This is Aunt Mabel's Red Hat group."

"Red Hat Group?"

She'd heard something about the group, but was unsure what the women did besides wear red hats. Feeling like it would be rude not to address the group at large, she did. "Sounds like you've had a great day."

"We did," a woman close to Elvin announced. "We saw a play, which was fair. We've had much more fun listening to your beau tell us about the unfolding of your romance."

Her eyebrows shot up to her hairline. Elvin coughed and cleared his throat before he spoke. "Ah, Agnes, you know no other woman can compare to you." He blew a kiss in the elderly woman's direction, causing her to giggle girlishly.

Distract and mislead was a technique Elvin had used on numerous occasions. He cupped Nala's elbow and steered her to a booth the farthest away from the whispering women. As soon as she sat, Elvin spoke. "Ignore Agnes. She gets confused easily. What can I get you to eat? My treat."

His treat? This day kept getting stranger and stranger. As a subcontractor, Elvin expected Nala to pay, but usually they ended up splitting the bill. His offer to pay shouted guilty. It made her wonder what tales he'd regaled the women with. It had to be something that made Aunt Mabel profoundly grateful.

"Hazelnut coffee and an orange scone."

"Will do." He threw her a mock salute and scurried off to the counter. Her eyes followed him while she wondered how she'd get him to recount whatever he said before her tardy entrance. Part of the reason Elvin was so important to her work was his superior intellect. He'd guess what she was up to. As a licensed investigator, she should have better ways to retrieve information.

A lengthy line developed at the counter, and Elvin was in the middle of it. Nala slipped out of her seat and strolled in the direction of Aunt Mabel. Out of the corner of her eye, she could see Elvin gesturing at her, but pretended not to.

She grabbed a straight back chair from another table. "Hello, ladies. Can I sit with you while Elvin gets our order?"

The women nodded and smiled. A few slid their chairs closer to each other, bumping hats, sending one of the feathery creations to the floor. Aunt Mabel waved her into the empty space.

"Hello, dear. My nephew failed to properly introduce us. I know he kept chattering about you. Nyla this, Nyla that, but he never mentioned your actual name."

"It's Nala." She enunciated it clearly, not wanting it confused with one of those Nyla bones made from mysterious materials that dogs could never ever wear away. "Nala Bonne."

"Oh, are you related to…"

She expected an inquiry about her father, Police Captain Spencer Bonne. Having served on the force for thirty years, most people had met him in some capacity or at least seen him in the paper or even on the news.

"…Gwen Bonne, the owner of Posh Interiors?"

This was a surprise. "Yes, I am."

There was flurry of remarks about her mother being Gwen Bonne.

"Love that place."

"It's so upscale."

"You're so lucky to have a mother who's a successful business woman and a fashion plate."

She smiled her third forced smile of the day. Life was grand as Gwen Bonne's daughter. People usually expected her to be as multi-talented as her mother. She'd given it a go, but unfortunately managed to be a mediocre preschool teacher and a struggling private eye. Her mother was always quick to give advice and offer a hand. Most might have taken the help eagerly, but it was important to Nala to accomplish things on her own. So far, she hadn't had any luck getting her parents to understand this.

Mabel reached over and patted her hand as she spoke. "Enough about your mother. I want to hear about you and Elvin."

The conversation was not going in the direction she wanted, but she'd already learned when it came to investigation that it was better to ramble a tiny bit, before redirecting to her desired question.

"I'm sure he told you how we met."

Mabel's penciled in eyebrows drew together. "Goodness. My

rapscallion nephew failed to mention it." She pressed both hands together in a prayer attitude. "Was it romantic?"

The possibility made Nala laugh. "Only if you consider high school chemistry romantic. Our teacher, Mrs. Janeway, thought the pairing of my best friend, Karly, and myself might turn out to be highly explosive since neither of us had a clue about balancing chemical formulas. She made us work with different partners and put me with Elvin, who happened to be an excellent partner."

"Oh." Aunt Mabel worked her mouth as if she tasted something sour and was not a fan of it. "That was so long ago."

The way Mabel emphasized so made it sound like it had been back when the dinosaurs had roamed the earth. "It wasn't that long ago."

"Ten years or close to it. If my nephew could have charmed you as well as he does women he has no interest in, then I would have had a grandniece or grandnephew by now, possibly both."

Grandniece or grandnephew? Elvin must have alluded to being much closer than they were. She'd suspected as much. Shouldn't be too shocking considering he took a snapshot of them when they first started working together. He claimed it would put his grandmother's mind at ease if she thought he was keeping company with an appropriate female. Even though she was not a fan of the idea, the image of a fragile elderly woman hanging onto life by a gossamer thread kept her from protesting too much.

"Elvin told me he was worried about his grandmother. Could that be your mother?"

"Possibly. Depends on how he described her."

"General concern about her health. This was a few months ago."

Her eyes rolled up as she tried to remember. One of her friends interjected. "Didn't your mother fall during the running of the weasels?"

"That's right. I almost forgot." Mabel shook her head. "It was a silly event her retirement home put on to mimic the running of the bulls, only with weasels. One of the low-slung devils tripped her. She caught herself before she hit the ground, but apparently it ruined her chance of winning. No bones were broken. In fact, she's on safari right now in Kenya. It's a camera safari where they shoot photos of the animals."

"Sounds like fun." It also sounded like Elvin had stretched the truth, unless he had another grandmother who was alive and well. "Maybe he was talking about his other grandmother."

"Evelyn? Technically, he was named after her. I consider the choice his father's influence." Her quarrelsome tone indicated the brother-in-law was not a favorite. "His mother used to be a hostess at one of those gambling casinos in Las Vegas. Still a looker, she must have married very young the first time. She and her fourth husband live somewhere in Arkansas now. Heard tell they run a quartz mining operation. It must be quite a change going from the glitter of Vegas to grubbing in the dirt. Wouldn't be too worried about Evelyn, unless Elvin was concerned about her habit of discarding husbands whenever she got a wild hair."

"Hmmm." Nala stalled as she searched for a tactful comment while not revealing Elvin had told her a tall one. The man in question strode to the table with a determined expression and white knuckling the plastic tray with the coffee and pastries he carried.

"I've got our order."

"I see." She waved at her red hat friends before making her way to their booth in the back.

Elvin moved closer and inquired in a faint voice. "Did you get any info from my aunt? I know that's what you went over there for."

Her lips twisted in a grimace as she realized the woman pulled quite a bit of information from her. "Not what I expected. I ended up telling her about how we met."

Elvin put down the tray on the table before slipping into his seat. He handed Nala her coffee and scone. "Should I ask what tidbit Aunt Mabel revealed that you will use to bludgeon me with when the occasion merits it?"

Instead of answering, Nala picked up her coffee and sipped the fragrant brew, enjoying the slightly sweet taste. She could tell Elvin how his fragile grandmother story had been busted, but she decided against it, wanting to see if the man would voluntarily confess or dig the hole even deeper.

"Nala, come on. I know Aunt Mabel. If gossip were an Olympic sport, she'd be a gold medalist." He planted both elbows on the table and leaned forward as if he could will her to tell.

Nope. It wasn't going to work. Her father had practiced different types of intimidation people might use. At the time she was entering middle school, her father feared some less than savory associates would influence her into listening to emo bands and dying her hair odd colors. The trick to intimidation was to redirect the intimidator's attention. Her hand slipped into her purse and pulled out the plastic baggie of the burnt ash from Fiona's fire.

"I need you to examine this. I have a client who is being harassed by an unknown person or persons. The last incident was starting a fire near her dog kennel."

Elvin held the bag at eye level. "What's so special about this?"

"That's your job. Go analyze it."

He shook the bag causing the ash to dissolve into even smaller pieces. "Looks like paper to me."

"That's what I thought. Still, there might be some distinctive accelerant on it that could help me determine who started it or get me going in the right direction." That was her plan. It would be cool to solve the case in less than a day. It would do a great deal for her credibility as a private eye. Fiona could recommend her to her friends, if she had any that weren't four-legged.

An acrid smell permeated the booth as Elvin opened the bag and sniffed. "Turpentine."

"I thought so, too. Still, that could be the base element. It could have been mixed with something else, too. It might be the calling card of a known arsonist."

Elvin pushed back from the table and slumped against the back of the booth seat. "Analyze it. I think that is more of the fire department's job. They have an arson squad. As for known arsonists, I would assume if they were known, then they'd be behind bars."

So much for her assumption that she'd hand Elvin the ash and he'd do the rest. "I need you to do this. The police had no interest in the case."

"Why is that?"

Ah, this would be a sticking point. She shrugged as if the entire issue somehow befuddled her. "Oh, it's hard to say. I wasn't there when the police officer responded to the call."

"Who was?" His gaze dropped to his fingers that were in the process of shredding an oversized cinnamon roll. He corralled a few shreds and stuffed them into his mouth.

"Karly was there."

"Yeah, she'd be a reliable source of information. She can be observant if not distracted by some homeless dog or an equally pathetic loser guy."

Nala reached across the table and gave Elvin a light punch.

"That's for your remark about my friend. Not all the guys she has interest in are pathetic." It made her wonder how he knew so much. Karly almost never associated with Elvin outside of attending school together.

He threw up his hands. "Forget about it." His impersonation of the movie gangster line fell a little flat. His insistence on using movie lines as hackneyed pickup lines had kept the man free of romantic entanglements.

"I trust my friend. She's not the problem. It may have been my client Fiona Bridgewater. The officer acted like he didn't accept the story. He took the statement and even the written threat, but Karly felt he acted like Fiona made up everything. Probably thought she was this crazy chick who wanted attention." She stopped her explanation to sip her coffee.

"Sounds about right."

His unexpected response resulted in her choking on her coffee. She placed the cup on the table as she wheezed for breath. Elvin came around the table to slap her on the back. His vigorous pounding didn't help. Eventually, she caught her breath, but Elvin remained seated beside her.

"Are you okay?" His concerned eyes held hers.

"Yeah, I'm good. What did you mean by sounds about right?"

"Oh, that. Fiona Bridgewater is known to be as crazy as a loon."

The woman she met had been abrupt, not terribly social, but to be fair she'd just experienced a shock. Crazy was not a word she'd apply to her. "What makes her crazy?"

"Besides building a Taj Mahal of a dog house out in the boondocks?"

"Elvin, you are aware that the Taj Mahal is a mausoleum?"

"No. I just thought it was a fancy place that people go to see.

Yeah, but she did build that super dog house."

"That she did, but lots of people love their dogs. There are people who send their dogs to day camp while they are at work. The dog bakeries, grooming salons, and pet clothes manufacturers do a big business. For Pete's sake, they have doggie ice cream. Are all those people bonkers?" Most would say she was looney tooney since she not only talked to her dog, but he answered.

He nodded, popped a bite of cinnamon roll into his mouth, and chewed as his eyes sparkled with mirth. Once he swallowed, he finally spoke. "I see I hit a sore spot. You're probably thinking about Max who is a pretty cool dude despite his four-legged status. I wouldn't mind babysitting him again. He's a real babe magnet. As for Fiona, before she inherited that bundle of money, you'd see her at the city-county building street corner holding up a sign that announced *Dogs Have Rights,* too. It seemed a shame to give all that lovely money to someone like that."

It was easy to make fun of someone who declared dogs had rights. Although she understood the intent that dogs should be treated as well as people as opposed to being abandoned, neglected, or abused. If Elvin knew about Fiona, it wasn't a far stretch to imagine whoever harassing her knew just as much, which meant it could be anyone. The thought killed her easy case theory.

"Do you think everyone knows this?"

"Depends. It's a local deal. Most people are getting their news from the Internet. I imagine there's at least a thousand or more locals who know, but few of them have the ability to recall the information and put it together in such a skillful way as I did."

Nala managed to maintain her expression of polite interest as she considered a thousand people knowing about Fiona and her obsession with rescue dogs. The possible suspects pool became obscenely large. "Do you know where Fiona lives?"

His eyes rolled upward as he asked, "Why do you ask? Did you tell me when you called? I assume she lives in Indianapolis. Right, kid. Here's looking at you." He shaped his thumb and forefinger into a L shape, pointed it at her and winked.

"Your Bogey impersonation could use work, and I don't like to be called kid." Although, it was preferable to the insinuation that Mabel had made that it had been a long time since she was a kid. If Elvin, whose natural curiosity and hacker tendencies allowed him to tiptoe through people's private matters, didn't know where Fiona lived, then who would?

"You have no respect for my art. What's up with the twenty questions?" He chased around the crumbs on his plate with a fingertip he had licked for such a purpose.

Nala inhaled as she pondered how much to tell. The private eye business was her dream. Both her mother and father wanted to give her advice on how to run her agency. She didn't need Elvin jumping in and giving his opinion, too, but it might be helpful.

"I'm conflicted. Fiona is my client, but I wonder if the note, phone calls, and even the fire could be a need for attention."

Elvin opened his mouth as if to speak, but Nala held up her hand to halt whatever he might say. "Karly and Fiona were both in the house together when the smoke alarms went off. There was no way Fiona could have set the fire."

"Okay. Do you think Fiona isn't behind everything?"

"I'm not sure. She could have paid a neighbor kid to set the fire. I will contact my father and see if he'll give me some info on the note the officer took. He might not, but Karly did take a photo of it."

"That could be useful. Can you send it to me? I've always wanted to try my hand at handwriting analysis."

The possibility cheered her. The rescue dog harasser might be back to a one-day case. Good, she needed a break. She had yet to turn the ringer back on her phone and it vibrated in her pocket, making her jump. A quick glance at caller ID told her it was Karly.

"What's happening?"

Her friend spoke so fast, punctuated by a sob, it was hard to understand her, but she thought she heard her right. To be sure, she decided to paraphrase the information. "Fiona Bridgewater is missing."

Chapter Eight

ELVIN INSISTED ON following her to Fiona's house, but she made a detour to pick up Max. Her large dog sat tall in the passenger seat as opposed to his usual riding style with his head out the window to sniff out a possible cheeseburger.

"It's about time you swung by and got me. I almost starved to death waiting on you."

Her rearview mirror showed Elvin was still behind her. Keeping her gaze straight ahead, so it wouldn't look like she was conversing with her dog, she answered his bogus claim. "I left you with plenty of kibble that was still in your bowl. Not sure how you could starve with all that food."

"It wasn't fresh. Would *you* want to eat stale food?"

"I have. Not sure if dog food can go stale. If you ate it right away instead of hanging out for something better it wouldn't be stale."

Max snorted and raised his nose a little higher as if offended. Her dog could be such a diva. She chose not to be taken in by his theatrics. "We're driving back to Fiona's to meet Karly. She thinks the rescue dog queen has been kidnapped."

"That wonderful woman! Who would do that?"

Wonderful woman might be overstating the case, but maybe she seems that way to dogs. "I'm not sure. Not even sure if she was truly kidnapped. Karly is in tears, and this is about as much as I could get out of her. She's at Fiona's place. Fiona isn't. She called the police, but they told her it was too soon to make a missing person's report since it had only been an hour."

"I thought you said kidnapping."

"I did because that's what Karly suspects, but there's no evidence of it so far. That's why we're all headed out to Fiona's place."

Instead of responding, Max stared straight ahead as they flashed by a series of fast food restaurants without even making a mention of them. Finally, he spoke. "What do you think?"

That was an excellent question. Obviously, the police officer hadn't taken Fiona seriously. Even though it didn't happen that much, police, judges, just people in general made mistakes. Those who put on a good front were perceived as not being dangerous, especially if they'd never been convicted. Then there were the eccentrics, who had probably cried wolf more than once. Due to their previous behavior, when they mentioned an issue, people tended to blow it off as a drug-induced hallucination or the product of an overactive imagination.

Often, the result of ignoring or being slow to answer such a call could be fatal. Her father insisted that every call should be treated as of the utmost importance. Most of his new graduates from the academy did so, but as the years passed, personalities emerged. There were those who felt they could read people better than her father, which led to them treating some calls as less important. Eventually, the information would make it back to the chief, who would take disciplinary measures, which resulted in a few seeking out different careers.

"I wish I knew. You're the one with the great nose. What can you tell me?"

"Are you asking for my opinion now?"

She recognized the tone of voice as a teasing one and glanced at her pooch who cocked his head and winked.

"I did ask."

"Fiona smelled honest. Authentic."

Could dogs actually tell if people were lying? If so, she could save a great deal of time on her online date investigation service if she could just get Max to give them the sniff test. Although, that would involve going out with the man or woman first with the plan to casually bump into Max and Nala. Most people wanted the potential candidate vetted before a date. "What does *honest* smell like?"

"It's more like what it doesn't smell like."

"You're talking in riddles now. Do you know or not?"

Bark! Bark! Bark!

Every now and then, Max slipped into dog speak. The weird thing was she was getting to the point she understood him. "Hey, I wasn't insulting you. Sorry."

He pointed his nose up and answered in an offended voice. "I might accept your apology."

"Geez! Could you get over yourself? A woman's life might hang in the balance." Personally, she wasn't even sure that Fiona had vanished. Maybe the woman had stopped at her favorite restaurant or spent a little extra time in a pet supply store. There was probably a reasonable explanation. The one thing she did know was that Max, for all his antics, did have a kind heart.

"Why didn't you say that in the first place?"

Before she could answer, he continued talking. "Scent carries a number of messages including everything or anyone you came into contact with. When people lie or pretend to be someone they aren't, they put out a bitter note in addition to whatever their regular scent is."

Had Jeff smelled differently toward the end of their relationship?

In retrospect, he had lied about many things. Nothing significant jumped out at her. Maybe he smelled the same because he was always being less than honest with her. Then again, maybe only dogs could sniff out deceit. "Dad always says amateur or impulsive perps sweat up a storm when you collar them. Does lying smell like sweat?"

"Ha! I know the smell of sweat. I live with you."

"Hey! I use deodorant."

Max smirked, letting her know she'd been played. "No, the smell isn't sweat. Sweat on humans smells slightly metallic. The lying smell is more bitter. It has a higher, lighter note than sweat on the scent scale."

"No full-bodied bouquet with a lingering aftertaste of grape-fruit?" she joked, acting as if his smell analysis was similar to a wine expert giving a summary of a particular vintage.

"Go ahead and make fun, but your nose hasn't come up with anything."

True. Her job had been mainly gathering clues, driving Max to various sites, getting Elvin to analyze the clues, and then interpreting the information she did have to come out with a probable conclusion. It may have been fate or luck, but so far, she'd closed every case she'd ever had. Five cases in all and one of them was finding a lost dog.

"You're right. My nose hasn't been good for much. Fortunately, my driving skills get you and your fabulous nose where we need to go."

She left the restaurant in such a hurry, she still hadn't turned the ringer on her phone and jerked when it vibrated again, interrupting any response Max might make. She assumed it was Karly. Nala thumbed the phone and put it on speaker. "Keep your panties on,

I'm almost there."

A masculine voice came over the phone speaker. "I'm not wearing any panties, but if I were why might I be keeping them on?"

The shock at hearing an unexpected voice sent her memory on full recall. Thank goodness it wasn't her father or Elvin. Elvin would have a heyday at her expense. It was neither Dad nor Elvin and at this time, no other males were calling her. She hesitated just long enough for Max to chime in.

"Tyler."

Oh fudge. It was Tyler, and Max had just talked again.

A deep chuckle came over the phone. "Nala, that thing you do when you pretend to talk with a man's voice is kinda amusing in person, but over the phone it's a little unsettling."

Nala shot her grinning pooch a look that promised retribution in the form of bypassing drive-thru restaurants that sold his beloved cheeseburgers if he kept talking for her. Nala turned off the speaker and cradled the phone between her ear and shoulder. Talking on the cell while driving could be problematic.

"Tyler. What a surprise."

"Obviously you were expecting someone else."

"Karly."

"That explains the panties part."

"Yeah." She had just seen the man this morning. Twice even. Normally, she would have given the prospect of a date with the handsome veteran turned cop a great deal of thought, but with her day so far, she hadn't. Instead, she had to wonder why he was calling. Didn't guys have some type of protocol for not calling right away? She wasn't sure of the exact time parameters, but how soon they called indicated how much interest they had in a woman. Men always appeared to be masters at pretending disinterest.

"Hey, I was wondering if you thought much about the burger you owe me."

"Well, I…" She hesitated, not knowing what to say. Nala had never been in a position where she held the power regarding a date. To say she'd been way too busy to give it a thought could be construed as insulting. Still, to say she'd thought about it would be a lie.

"Don't bother lying to me. I will tell you that *I* have thought about it. How about tonight? Nothing fancy."

"Ah, that sounds nice, but I'm on a case. Max and Elvin are driving out to the site with me now. Not sure if I'll be free tonight. Maybe tomorrow night?"

"Un-huh. Isn't Elvin that obnoxious geeky guy from your previous case? The one who knew you were in trouble before everyone else did. He also called you his girl."

His girl? She had no clue that Elvin had done that. It also explained why Tyler had immediately lost interest in her after the case. "Elvin is a subcontractor I work with on occasion. If he ever called me his girl, it had to be a joke. Maybe you misheard."

"A guy notices when another man speaks that way about a woman. I'll take your word that the two of you aren't involved romantically."

"That's good of you." She meant it sarcastically, but since the comment was void of the appropriate snarky tone, even her zings turned out sounding like compliments.

"I know. Give me a call when you're free." There was a crackle and a murmur of a voice. "Got a call. Over and out."

Nala wasn't sure if he was talking to her or the police radio. She murmured bye and thumbed off the call. Instead of being delighted that Tyler had called, she felt slightly befuddled, not sure how she felt. Most women would be taken in by his broad shoulders or soulful eyes. No one would call him charming, but he wasn't a jerk either, which was a plus. *Strange.* She took his comment about taking her word that Elvin and she weren't romantically involved as slightly patronizing. Her mother would warn her that she picked things part. Her father would assure her Tyler was an outstanding officer. She blew out a long breath. "Don't overthink this."

Max turned his head her way and asked, "Overthink what?"

"Never mind."

Even Einstein talked to himself. It was a time-honored way of thinking over things. Something about hearing the actual words fired up your neurons or something. Answers you couldn't previously access showed up. She'd ask herself what to do about Elvin but knew whatever he had said a few months ago had already been forgotten. It would end up making her look needy as if she wanted a love connection. No thank you.

Back when they were in high school, girls generally avoided Elvin. He never comprehended that his intellectual humor didn't win him chicks who had no clue what he was talking about. The school jocks broke more than one pair of his glasses, certain that when he used words they didn't know he was somehow insulting them in code, when he really wasn't talking about them at all. About that time, he resorted to his movie talk and impressions. Although it could be irritating trying to converse with him while wondering if he was giving a real answer or a movie quote, it had saved his parents money in replacing glasses. At last, he'd found a way to connect with the general populace. Like most things he did, Elvin overdid it.

Nala shook off the idea that Elvin could be romantically interested in her. He was like that with every woman he met. He acted as if he were immediately smitten no matter who the woman was and poured on the flattery. Most were icked out by the show. A few saleswomen or waitresses grudgingly endured it. People like his aunt's friends good-naturedly accepted it. Come to think of it, he didn't over compliment her. Her lips twisted to one side as she considered some of their conversations. Nope, none of them could be considered romantic in the least. It was more like friends or a brother and sister.

As if he knew she was thinking about him, Elvin inched up closer in his flashy orange Dodge Charger and honked his horn twice. Nala glanced in her rearview mirror and saw his grin. He thought he was being funny. Yeah, he was like an annoying brother.

Chapter Nine

THE BLACK AND white cows grazing in a green field signaled the dairy she used as a marker, which meant not much longer to Fiona's place. Elvin had dropped back from his earlier position, but was close enough to see her turn signal. Whenever a Tipton resident was near the road, they always waved. Nala waved back wondering if they mistook her for someone else or if the folks were just friendly.

The lavish home that had been lit up last night appeared less like a celestial event in the daylight. It still could have served as a small hotel. She needed to look for the blue mailbox before she turned.

The unmarked dirt drive meandered through the overgrown brush. Both Elvin and Nala crept up Fiona's road. She drove slowly, hoping to discover a clue she could have missed in the dark. Elvin probably drove slow to protect his fancy car. Then again, he had no choice since he was behind her.

Nala nudged Max. "Keep alert. There may be a clue out there we're missing."

Her dog leaned away from her. "Stop poking me! I can't smell while we're traveling. I'm not a bloodhound."

"Point taken. When we get there, I need you to sniff around for Fiona and anyone who could have possibly taken her."

"I will be glad to assist, if you address me as Officer Max. I'd also like it if you conveyed my orders in the form of your mission, and then state the objective.

Nala shook her head and grumbled to herself. "I really have to talk to my father about his training methods."

"I'm waiting."

It might have been easy to command a dog who couldn't talk, but a dog that could speak like a human and had an attitude was much more difficult. It was easier to go along if she wanted anything done fast. "Officer Max, your mission is to sniff out the culprit who may have taken Fiona Bridgewater."

"Orders accepted. Will do." He lifted one paw and swiped at the air.

"What are you doing?"

"A snappy salute. It doesn't work well with a canine limb."

"Ah, yeah I see that now. We're here."

Karly stood at the open gates, wringing her hands. She ran toward the Volkswagen Beetle. "You're here!"

"Your crime-solving team has arrived. Let me park." She parked the car near Karly's wagon. Elvin parked next to her and managed to exit his car before Nala could hers. He opened the door for Max who leaped out and began strolling the area with his nose to the ground.

Elvin and Karly were already chatting when Nala reached them. Before she could ask what happened, Elvin spoke.

"The issue here is Fiona never returned home after telling Karly she'd meet her back here after the lawyer visit."

Karly nodded her head in vigorous agreement as Elvin summarized the situation. "Your friend called the police, who took the information, but stated they couldn't even label Fiona as a missing person until a little longer. They definitely couldn't call it a kidnapping without a ransom demand or any evidence of foul play. However, Karly thinks different." Elvin folded his arms and lifted one eyebrow as if daring Nala to comment on his assessment.

Karly ran to Nala who hugged her agitated friend. She held onto the trembling body, knowing that whatever had happened to Fiona, Karly believed it was foul play. "Hey, I know this is upsetting, but we're here now and will figure this out."

"I hope so. Thank goodness you brought Max."

Why did people keep assuming Max was the key to solving everything? All he did was tell her what he smelled. He apparently had the extra skill of detecting liars, but she hadn't put that to use yet. Truthfully, all she had was his word on his liar detection ability. She'd stopped by to pick up her pet from home, not for him to work the scene, but knowing he would fuss if she left him behind. There was also the bonus that she preferred traveling to unknown areas with her intimidating looking canine. Only those who knew Max well realized he was about as threatening as a kitten.

"He's hard on the job checking out the area."

Karly loosened her grip on Nala and stepped back. She put her hand up to shade her eyes and peered around the area. She pointed to Max. "When he's done, could you have him talk to the dogs again? Maybe they know something."

Elvin's mouth dropped open, indicating he'd heard. He moved a little closer. "You mean Max questions the dogs?"

Karly's lips parted, but Nala put her hand over her friend's mouth. In her agitated state, there'd be no telling what Karly might say. "Yeah, question the dogs." Nala forced herself to laugh. "That was more for Fiona than anything else. The woman loved her dogs."

Karly placed a hand on Nala's arm. "You said *loved*. Do you think Fiona is dead?" The hand on her arm tightened with the nails biting into her skin.

She shook free of her friend's grasp. "It was a grammar mistake. Sue me. It meant nothing. I've had very little sleep in the last twenty-four hours."

In the scheme of things, she should be the person freaking. She'd had too much stress and too little sleep, but that would require more energy than she currently possessed. Out of the corner of her eye, she saw Max sitting very straight with his ears erect. It was his report posture, another training technique courtesy of her father. She held up one finger to both Karly and Elvin. "Excuse me."

She hurried over to Max, worried what trouble would happen by allowing her two friends to converse with each other without her serving as a monitor to steer them away from personal subjects such as her talking dog or lack of a love life. Oh, well, she'd worry about it later. She knelt beside Max, not wanting Elvin to notice she was talking to Max, although plenty of people did talk to their dogs.

"What did you find?"

Max dipped his head and said, "Officer Max."

Snickerdoodles! Her father would pay for this. She had no clue how, but he would. "Officer Max, report."

"Yes, sir. Perimeter patrolled. No sign of Fiona Bridgewater. Scent trail is old. She hasn't been here since early morning."

That wasn't helpful. It was the same information Karly had already relayed to her. If someone did kidnap Fiona, her isolated home would be the perfect place if the alarm system was turned off. Why would the system be turned off, though? If anything, she'd expect the woman to be extra cautious after the fire.

"Anyone else?"

"Old smell of you. Karly, of course. No one else."

The night before they had investigated the site of the fire. "What about the scent of the man you smelled who had started the fire?"

"That wasn't me. I think Twinkle Toes mentioned she felt the essence of a man or something like that."

It was an entirely different thing to have confidence in someone else's dogs. It could be the fire and the vanishing of Fiona weren't necessarily connected. Maybe Karly had misunderstood Fiona's directives. Nala loved her friend, but knew too much stress could weird her out. When her friend had taken too many AP classes in high school, she spoke with a horrible cockney accent but insisted she didn't.

Even though most people wouldn't consider being entrusted with the security code, being named as an heir in Fiona's will, and being given the power of attorney as especially nerve-wracking, it would be to Karly. She counted it a measure of personal growth that her friend wasn't speaking with a cockney accent yet.

Elvin slipped up behind her and bent slightly at the waist, putting his hands on his knees. "What has Scooby-doo come up with?"

Max pointed his nose up, a thing he did when put out. Apparently, he did not appreciate being compared to a cartoon character.

"Nothing new. Fiona hasn't been here since morning."

Elvin arched his eyebrows. "You know this how?"

It was a perfectly reasonable question. "Ah, I'm sure you've heard there are psychic bonds between pets and their owners?" She could feel Max stiffen beside her. He disliked the use of the word owner.

Elvin shook his head. "Yeah, I heard about it, but with me not having a pet it would be hard for me to comment on it. So, you're saying while I was talking to Karly, you and Fido were having a Vulcan mind meld."

Leave it to Elvin to make her bogus claim sound even more outrageous than having a talking dog. It was hard to know how to explain it better. Max stood and growled menacingly.

Elvin backed away holding his hands out. "Hey, boy, I thought you and I were friends. Remember the T-bone I grilled for you?"

Here she'd been blaming her father for Max's picky dining habits. Apparently, the one time she allowed Elvin to babysit, he hadn't stuck to the provided nutritionally correct kibble. Nala pointed to her friend who was walking backwards. "You're the one who made Max such a picky eater!"

Elvin shook his head, although his denial didn't float. He'd already admitted to giving her pet a steak. "C'mon. Call off Rin Tin Tin. I'm sorry about the steak. If anything, the dog should love me."

Nala slipped her hand down by her side and waved at her pet to stop his growling. It wasn't any agreed upon signal, but somehow Max knew what she wanted, which probably meant they did have a psychic connection.

Elvin returned back to Karly's side, and the two of them had their heads together speaking in low voices, making Nala walk a little faster. As she came closer, she heard Karly respond.

"I did call Fiona, several times. It doesn't even ring but goes directly into voice mail. Peculiar."

Elvin stroked his chin in what Nala recognized as his thoughtful pose. *Fudge!* He could have answered immediately, but instead he was giving Karly time to observe his profile. Elvin once confessed to her during chemistry class that he thought he had a classic profile. At the time, she said nothing because she really needed Elvin as a lab partner to pass the class. Was he hitting on Karly? She didn't need that. Worse, the man was asking questions she'd just thought of. Not willing to be outfoxed by her subcontractor, Nala chimed in.

"Her phone must be dead or off."

"The police did mention that as a possibility.

Karly turned away from Elvin and rolled her eyes upward. On the way back, she'd call her father to ask him to look into the situation. Right now, she needed to ask the right questions. "Did the police say anything else to you?"

Karly pursed her lips before answering. "They told me to wait a while and call back later if she didn't show. The dogs are fed twice a day. They were fed this morning, and they are usually fed around six, which isn't too far off. I need to stay here to make sure the dogs are fed tonight."

"What are you going to do about work?"

"I'm hoping Fiona will come back tonight, and it has all been a big mistake. The police did mention if she had her car, purse, and was a functioning adult—which she is—she could be anywhere."

Yeah, that's what Nala wanted. Fiona could come tripping in, laden down with dozens of dog sweaters she just bought. It would help if Nala discovered the harasser was a prankster as opposed to a sociopath. Even still, charges could be pressed, even though he'd probably get off with only probation.

"You could feed the dogs, go home, and come back the next day if needed."

Elvin nodded in agreement. "Yeah, you don't want to stay here. It's not clear if whoever is harassing Fiona is after her or just wants to get rid of the dogs."

Oh, he didn't! Leave it to Elvin to go to the worst-case scenario. He had to mention a danger to the dogs. Karly's anxious expression became a little more pronounced.

Until she met Fiona, she would have sworn that Karly was the biggest dog lover she'd ever met. She probably had a dog suit with a big SDR on it for Super Dog Rescuer hidden in the back of her closet. Any mention of dogs in distress would send her friend rushing out in the middle of the night.

Elvin kept talking despite Nala mouthing the words *shut up.*

"What if the man decides to blow the place to kingdom come? Pow!" He gestured, throwing his hands upward, pantomiming an explosion.

Oh, great, now he's done it.

Karly pressed both hands against her chest. "I can't leave these dogs here on their own. I can't take them home, either. As a trustee, I have to stay."

Fig bars! Karly had a point, and she'd not dissuade her. The only thing she could do was find Fiona Bridgewater.

"All right, Elvin, get to work on that ash. I'll stay with Karly."

The two of them stood together and waved at Elvin as he drove away. Once he drove out of sight, Nala turned to her dog.

"Officer Max."

She waited until Max sat at attention before proceeding.

"Your mission is to question the residents of the canine hotel." The name was one she coined for the glorified kennel.

"Ready as ordered. Can you open the door for me?"

"Will do." She strolled with the dog over to the kennel with Karly following.

The rescue dogs greeted Max with friendly yips and barks. The women closed the door on the scene and returned to the house.

"Do you think we should stay so we can open the door for Max?"

Nala shrugged her weary shoulders. "Otis can open the door. He's a boxer and can use his paws like hands."

Her friend nodded in agreement. "I keep forgetting that. What about your preschool job? You hardly got any sleep last night."

"Don't I know it? My body aches all over. I think I feel a sick day coming on. Let's hope Fiona has something decent for human consumption in her fridge."

Chapter Ten

FIONA'S KITCHEN TABLE was littered with half-empty coffee cups and a pizza box left from the night before. The whiteboard was still balanced against the telephone books and the yellow legal tablets were still in their place.

Karly wrinkled her nose as she picked up the coffee cups. "Fiona isn't much of a house keeper."

"Yeah, I noticed." She picked up the pizza box. Her stomach gave an audible growl sensing food. Lifting the lid, she discovered a congealed pizza slice. Before she could decide what to do with her find, Karly yanked the box from her.

"Have some pride. You're not a frat boy. I'll fix you some real food."

Twenty minutes later, with the kitchen tidied, Karly stood at the stove stirring pasta sauce. "Remember our girls' nights?"

"Yeah. Before Bethany got married and Simone dropped out."

"Ah, yeah, I heard Simone got married, too."

"When did that happen?"

Karly shrugged her shoulders. She must not have received a wedding invite, either. No matter, it would have probably been a destination wedding Nala couldn't afford to attend. Simone was all about appearances and wouldn't have quietly married at the courthouse.

"Here we are, just like before." She didn't need to mention the fact that they were holding a watch for Fiona or whoever might try to harm the rescued dogs. Come to think of it, it was probably a good idea for someone outside of Elvin to know where she was. She dialed her father's number without mentioning her intentions to Karly.

Her father answered on the first ring. "Are you in danger?"

"Is that how you answer all your calls?"

"Not all, but I knew it was you."

Her mother called out in the background. "Does Nala need help?"

"Tell Mom I don't need help." She lowered her voice as if her mother might eavesdrop. "I'm on a case and thought you need to know what is going on in case something happens."

Her father cleared his voice. "Is this besides Fiona Bridgewater might be missing?"

"How did you know that?" Her father should be running the FBI or CIA with his connections. "Were you reading the daily reports?"

"I did see Karly's name and knew you'd be close."

"Okay, here's the deal. Someone is harassing Fiona. Left a note on her car, threatening phone calls, and last night a fire on her property."

"Yeah, I read that report, too."

"What's your take?"

"You're asking for my opinion?"

Max had nailed her father's tone when he asked her the same question before. "Yes, I am."

"Good answer. I'd like to see the note. If nothing else, I could send it through handwriting analysis software."

"You already have it. The reporting Officer Daylen took it with him. It should be in the evidence locker."

"Okay. I'll get on it. So, where are you?"

"I'm at Fiona's house with Karly. She's hopefully waiting for Fiona's return or a ransom note or call. I didn't want her to be alone, especially since Elvin implied staying at the house could be dangerous."

"Elvin's right. Why are you staying there?"

"Twenty-one dogs. Would you like to house twenty-one dogs?"

A bark of laughter erupted from her cell. Nala pulled the phone away from her ear since her father was a loud laugher. Finally, he wound down and managed to speak in an amused tone. "Can you imagine how your mother would react with all those dogs in the house?"

It wasn't hard considering her mother barely tolerated both her and her father inside the immaculate home. "It wouldn't make you too popular."

"You, either."

"You're right. Just wanted to let you know what was going on. I know this is far out of your district, and I don't expect you to pull any strings. I feel someone should know."

"In case anything went wrong."

She had thought that, but hearing him voice her thoughts created a heavy sensation in her stomach. "Just trying to be thorough."

"I understand."

"Thanks, Dad. I'll call later."

"Do that."

Nala ended the call feeling somewhat better. Elvin was out doing his job with the ashes. Her father would run the handwriting analysis while she stayed here waiting. The culprit could be watching them right now waiting for the perfect moment. She jumped up, causing the kitchen chair she had been using to fall backward.

"Karly!"

Her friend spun from her place at the stove, holding a wooden spoon dripping tomato sauce. "What?"

The possibility that they both could have been guilty of doing something so obviously stupid made it hard to speak. "I know we closed the gate after Elvin left, but did you enable the security system?"

The dripping spoon dropped to the floor, which answered her question. Karly rushed to a panel on the wall and punched out a quartet of numbers to turn on the security system. The system could be activated from the house while the gate had to be opened or closed by the outside controls, which meant the gate was added later, probably when the kennel was built. Nala closed her eyes and curled her toes, to stop herself from screaming in frustration. She needed sleep and food that didn't consist of caffeine and sugar.

If there was an evildoer in their midst, he could be inside the gates, perhaps even in the kennel. Nala knew she'd have to check it out. The handgun her father insisted she carry as an investigator was tucked into her glove compartment since the administration frowned upon teachers carrying weapons. While most people would have worried about harried teachers threatening the students, it was more likely the teachers might wave the gun about when talking to the administrators. All in all, there was never a good reason for a gun in a school. Some of her students arrived with no sense of boundaries and went through her purse until she started locking it up, which hadn't slowed down the more enterprising ones.

All she had to do was go out to her car and get it. At least it wasn't dark. "I'll be right back. I'm going out to my car."

"Do you think you should?" Karly placed a staying hand on her arm. "It might not be safe."

The blare of the doorbell caused Karly's hand to clench on Nala's arm. The prospect of the possible culprit lingering outside the door made her gulp. Use your brain. Don't rush into anything. Think it through. Her father's favorite sayings returned, reminding her of what she needed to do.

Nala firmed her jaw, shook off Karly's restraining hand, and picked up her courage that had dropped somewhere around her ankles. Between the two of them, she was the only one trained in defensive techniques. If she could make it to her car, she'd have a gun. Her last defense class had emphasized using what was available around her. A quick glance revealed some cleaning supplies crowded on a counter. Nala withdrew the can of bug spray, certain that spraying it into the eyes of an attacker would be painful.

Her finger on the nozzle, she approached the door, adopting the stern, no-nonsense face she practiced in the mirror every day before the students arrived. She lowered her voice into what she felt was an authoritative tone. "Okay, hold your horses. I'm coming."

Bark! Bark!

It sounded like Max. She peered through the peephole to see her dog seated outside the door. He gave another bark, then looked over his shoulder. It looked like her dog and sounded like her dog. Nala swung the door open. "Get in here. What's with the barking?"

"I recognized your tone of voice and didn't want to be sprayed with anything yucky."

Even her dog knew she was predictable. Max paraded past her none too fast and waited in the short foyer. Once the door clicked shut, he swung his head left and right and asked in a whisper, "Where's the old one?"

"I'm not sure. Gus hasn't been around since I entered the house. We could ask Karly."

"Don't bother. I try not to speak in human tongue while they're around. Dogs see it as a form of treason."

Treason. That seemed like the wrong word, but who knows what dogs really thought, especially as a group. "I don't think anyone with four legs can hear you. What did the dogs have to say?"

"I think I'll sit for the retelling." He suited his actions to his words and plopped down by Nala's feet. "Nothing good. Petunia is tired of the sensitive stomach dog food she's on. Told me it was bland, bland, bland. She'd like something with a little bacon grease in it."

She held up her hand before she got a recital on every dog's food preference. "I don't need to know who likes what for dinner."

Max gave a sharp bark of protest.

"What?"

"They haven't got their dinner yet. I thought you'd want to know their preferences especially since they might be off their food due to their pack leader not being present."

That's probably why the older dog was hiding out, possibly protesting the loss of his pack leader. She held up her hand, indicating Max should wait as she fetched paper and a pen. "Go ahead. I'll write the requests down and confer with Karly. Some of the dogs may be on a special diet for their health. Then we can feed them. Before we do that, is there any information pertinent to Fiona?"

"King Phillip told me he was watching a *M*A*S*H* rerun when they were fed breakfast."

"That should be easy enough to document. Anything else?" She'd assume that Fiona would have fed the dogs about the same time every day.

"Fiona started her car to leave while a Godzilla movie was on. King Phillip stated the monster hadn't made an appearance yet."

The relaxed German shepherd mix abandoned his lounging posture and immediately sat at attention.

It didn't take a mind reader to understand Max realized he had divulged facts without the proper protocol. "Please proceed, Officer Max."

"As ordered. The next entry came when The Beverly Hillbillies were on."

She noted the show, thinking it was probably Karly who had arrived. "Anything else?"

"There was the arrival of two more cars and the departure of one during the Wonder Woman movie starring Lynda Carter. King Phillip has a fondness for comic book characters."

"I noticed. I assume the cars were us and Elvin."

"That's what I thought."

"There was no screaming or yelling in German."

"None today."

It made her wonder if Officer Daylen had pegged Fiona better than she had. Didn't matter. A job was a job, and Fiona had written her a check. Her best bet was to cash it while she could. As a private investigator, her job wasn't to judge her clients, but to provide a service.

"Okay. Thank you, Officer Max. You might seek out Gus some-where in the house and see how he's doing."

"I'm on it." His nails clattered on the bare floor as he maneu-vered his way through the house.

Nala watched Max leave and regretted sending him off to find Gus when she should have insisted that he escort her to the car. It was still quite bright outside. With no known reason to fear anything, she exited the house and broke into a jog to the car. She could use the exercise or at least that is what she told herself.

Her weapon was buried under a wad of fast food napkins. After locating it, she checked the safety—on as it should be—and tucked the weapon into the waistband of her pants. Her father had mentioned more than once the dangers of transporting a weapon tucked in your waistband. There were always stories about people accidentally shooting themselves in the buttocks. Although it was never a fatal wound as far as the body went, a person's credibility took a major hit, but walking into the house, clutching a gun probably wouldn't do much for Karly's state of mind.

Once in the house, she kept the weapon by her leg and headed immediately for her purse to conceal the gun. That way she'd have it and not alarm her friend by an open display. Her dog loving friend was a total pacifist and believed the world would be a better place without weapons. Nala didn't disagree but knew a slimy sort of criminal would not be deterred by her shouting to halt in the name of justice. At this point, she hadn't used the gun in her investigation work at all. Last time she used it was at the firing range. Her father had joined her for practice, and she'd gone through two clips. *Ginger snaps!* Did she bother to reload her gun or had she just shoved it into the glove compartment? Nala reached for her firearm, but knew as soon as she pulled it free of her waistband what she feared was true. She should have paid more attention when she first picked it up, but speed had been her priority. It felt too light to be loaded. Just to be sure she pulled out the clip. *Nothing.* Not even a single bullet rested in the clip.

"What are you doing?" Karly asked.

The unexpected question startled her, making her juggle her weapon. It went airborne for a second, but Nala dropped to one knee before the expensive gun hit the floor. "Got it."

"You have a gun?" Karly's voice went up as she stated the obvious.

It didn't seem like a question worth answering, but knowing her friend's fears the least she could do is try to calm her. "No need to worry. Apparently, I forgot to reload the clip."

A small snort sounded as Karly shook her head and balled one hand on her hip. "What good is it then?"

Wait a minute. Did those words come out of Karly's mouth? "Who are you, and what have you done with my friend?"

"Be real. I just don't like senseless violence. All these kids shooting each other by mistake, because they're either showing off or stumbled onto their parents' guns. I don't approve stashing a handgun under the car seat so they can flash it around whenever someone doesn't do what they want. I sure don't approve of concealed weapons in public places such as shopping malls and concerts, but we have a situation here. There are almost two dozen lives at stake."

Had she missed something? Nala blinked and checked the safety on her weapon before tucking it back into her waistband. Sure, it was silly to check when she was out of bullets, but habit was habit. "Only Fiona is missing. We're not even sure she is missing. What's this about almost two dozen lives?"

"The dogs, of course."

Max trotted into the room, sat, and cocked his head, giving them both the look that shouted his confusion about human actions. Even though his expression made her want to laugh, she continued her conversation with Karly.

"Oh, yeah, that's right. How could I have forgotten?" Nala made a point of ignoring her friend's raised eyebrows and open mouth as she headed toward the kitchen.

Max barked once. Oh, yeah, she had sent him off on a mission.

"You find Gus?"

Nothing. No response. Yeah right. She forgot how he wanted to be addressed. "Officer Max. Report."

He sat up a little straighter. "Officer Max reporting. The subject, Gus, is curled up on a bathrobe in the bedroom. He's awake, but uncommunicative."

"Thank you, Officer Max." At least that answered the question where Gus had disappeared to. "Is dinner fixed yet?"

Karly gave a short nod. "It is. That's what I came to tell you when I caught you with the gun."

The accusatory tone made it sound like she'd done something wrong. Nala followed her friend into the kitchen as she explained. "It *is* my gun, which I need for my investigations."

"I get that, but what good is it without bullets?"

Max padded after them. "Girls, girls, that will be enough."

Snickerdoodles! Her dog was starting to sound like her mother. He managed to inject that long-suffering tone always present in her mother's speech whenever someone was doing something she didn't like. The last thing she needed was a dog who could mimic her mother. Next thing he'd be doing is giving her fashion advice and warning her if she wasn't on her A game at all times, she'd never meet Mr. Right or possibly even Mr. Good Enough.

Chapter Eleven

KARLY CLEARED A section of the table and placed a couple of plastic placemats with cartoon bones all over them. They may have not been meant for humans, but rather to go under dog bowls. Nala decided not to comment. She wanted to eat tonight, and it did smell appetizing.

"Anything I can do to help?"

Her friend portioned out the spaghetti onto the plates as she answered. "I have two side salads in the fridge. I did have some wine, but you'll have to forgo it if you have to drive back and get bullets."

Drive back and get bullets. Did she have any clue how long of a drive that was? Besides, she wasn't entirely sure if she left the backup ammo at the house or the office. "I couldn't leave you alone."

Certain the possibility of being left alone would do the trick, Nala allowed herself a small smile as she placed the salads on the table.

"No worries. Max can stay with me, and there is a security system. I have my phone and I can always call Elvin or that hottie in blue that has a suggestive name. What was it?"

Gosh, she must have the memory of an elephant, and Karly also knew good and well what the name was, but would make Nala say it.

"Goodnight. Officer Goodnight. Are you happy?"

Karly carried the plates, trailing the spicy scent of spaghetti sauce and meatballs. First, she placed them on the table and centered them on the mats, before smirking. "Yeah, that did make me a little happy. Max mentioned you bumped into him today."

The dog in question had been sitting near the table with his nose very close to one plate. "Max!"

He jumped to his feet and backed up a few steps before protesting. "Come on, I wasn't going to take the first bite. I'd be content with the second or third."

"There'll be no bites, unless they're last bites." She turned to address her friend. "When did you two talk?"

"When you went out to your car. Let me get the garlic toast and we can eat." Karly wrapped a dish towel around her hand, opened the oven door, and lifted out the fragrant bread.

Once the toast had been relocated to the table, the women sat down to eat. Max stood about a foot away looking woebegone. Karly tossed a piece of toast in his direction that he snapped out of the air.

Nala twisted in her chair ready to warn her pooch not to gobble his food, but it was too late.

"Tell me about you and Officer Goodnight."

"How about I don't tell you." Nala took a huge bite of her bread and chewed. Eventually, her friend would expect her to say something, but outside of the facts, which she was sure Max had already related, there wasn't much to tell, except for her absolute ambiguity about the entire matter. When in doubt, change the subject. "Did you hear about the clown sightings?"

Her friend speared a meatball and gestured with her laden fork as she spoke. "Oh, that again. It's not even Halloween. Some joker thinks it's a real hoot to dress up like a clown and stand beside a street just to be sure of being seen."

"Yeah, something like that." Nala concentrated on twirling the spaghetti around her fork as opposed to shoveling the food in with both hands, which she was tempted to do. Her frozen lunch entrée hadn't thawed as much as she had wanted and an unexpected phone call from a parent who'd heard about the advertisement for preschool position kept her from grabbing the microwave first. By the time she reassured the mother that she wasn't leaving due to some gossip she'd heard about a family curse, all the microwaves were not only busy, but there was a line, too. She made an attempt to eat the half-frozen stuffed pepper, but it stuck in her throat along with the idea of a family curse.

Her curses were probably no worse than clowns. It might be a bit unfair playing the clown card as a distraction, knowing how her friend felt about them. She knew Karly wasn't afraid of them, but she wasn't amused by them, either.

"Another thing about clowns." Karly gestured so vigorously that the meatball flew off her fork, but was caught by the ever opportunistic Max. Her friend looked momentarily distressed, but continued speaking. "Clowns paint on these faces that don't represent who they are. A clown with a happy face could be clinically depressed. Is that even fair?"

"To whom?"

"Well…" She paused and appeared thoughtful. "I was going to say the audience. Maybe it isn't fair to the clown. If people expect clowns to be funny all the time, do they ever get any down time?"

"I'm sure they do." Nala hadn't mean to conduct a deep discussion on the downfalls of being a clown. "All they have to do is take off their makeup and put on their street clothes. No one would ever recognize them in the grocery. Not like my parents, who think it is perfectly fine to have an impromptu conference in the frozen food section."

Max moved a little closer to the table, since he'd already snagged two airborne edibles. Nala caught the movement in her peripheral vision, but she pretended not to. If she acted like she saw him, he would take that as a yes and he could do whatever he just did. The dog played a constant game of opposite day, a game enjoyed by her preschoolers of doing or saying the exact opposite of what you should do.

"Since you cooked, I'll help you feed the dogs, then do the dishes."

Karly, still chewing, shook her head.

"Okay, then. I'll feed the dogs and do the dishes, while you watch television."

"No." Karly spoke around a bit of bread and then swallowed. "I can do the dishes and feed the dogs. I don't mind. I need you to go buy bullets, fetch them or whatever."

They were back to that again. The last thing Nala wanted was to drive anywhere. The office was a little closer. She did leave her laptop there, after Harry had been kind enough to help her with a graphics program she'd bought. The program had been his idea, and he'd felt obliged to make sure it worked.

Nala had cleared most of her plate when the brain storm hit. She brandished a finger. "I have an idea."

"Let's hear it."

"I've been working on the assumption that whoever is harassing Fiona is someone she knows."

"Makes sense."

"What if it isn't? What if it's someone she knows minimally at best?"

"That would make it difficult."

"I know." Which was why she had zero suspects so far. "What if you've seen or met the harasser?"

"Doesn't seem likely, considering my job."

"Keep thinking about people you have met while with Fiona. When I pick up my bullets, I'll get my laptop, which has a facial construction program on it. I can develop a possible sketch or sketches of people of interest."

"Hmm, sounds interesting." Karly put both elbows on the table and leaned in Nala's direction. "Let's say we can come up with some sketches. It's not like you're going to turn them over to your father to identify."

The police data base would be helpful, but as a private citizen she didn't have access to it. "Not hardly. In the end, the police tend to look at the data base containing previous offenders."

"Makes sense. It's what I would do."

Most of her cases had included solid research, but usually she'd unearthed her culprit by an epiphany that could occur anywhere or the suspect could be chasing her and firing at her, which was always a dead giveaway. Her hunch told her that whoever they were looking for wouldn't be a career criminal, although her hunches weren't always timely. Her mother sometimes referred to her great grandmother having 'the sight.' The woman who had died before Nala ever got to know her could accurately predict who was on the phone before she picked it up. Great Grandmother Esme just knew things she had no way of knowing. Nala hoped she may have gotten a pinch of the mental magic.

Nala shook her head slightly. "I'd agree with you normally, but it doesn't feel right."

"How should it feel?"

The problem with hunches is they weren't that easy to explain. Using the last bit of her garlic toast, Nala mopped up the remaining sauce on her plate. "Well, I did think about it coming over here."

"And?"

"How long has Fiona been getting calls and such?"

Karly's fork hovered halfway to her mouth as her eyes rolled upward. "I'm not totally sure. I guess the last two or three months. I met Fiona when she came to pick up the dogs. She never even mentioned anything about being harassed until a couple of weeks ago. From her comment, I got the idea it had been going on for a while."

"All right, consider a known felon, someone who has done time and is probably not anxious to do any more. Would he prolong a harassment campaign knowing at any time the police or," she pointed her thumb back at herself, "a private investigator could be called in?"

"I see your point." Karly reached for her glass and sipped her water. "Who would bother to do all of this?"

"That's the million-dollar question." She waggled her eyebrows as she continued, "My first conclusion is a crazy person. We have plenty of those as the clown sightings demonstrate. These are people who aren't really dangerous, but are determined to make a statement."

"What about the teens? Fiona initially thought it was someone goofing around."

Max propped his head on the table. "I didn't smell any of that overpowering spray by the remains of the fire."

At Karly's confused look, Nala explained. "Max assumes all teens douse themselves in body spray since one of my neighbor's grandsons does. He tried to pat Max, which resulted in my partner backing away because he couldn't take the smell."

"Okay. I get it. We also keep referring to the culprit as he. What if it isn't?"

Having experienced Fiona up close and personal, she could see her offending both male and female alike. "You have a point. What if this isn't one person?"

"A gang!" Karly slapped both hands on either side of her face resembling the scream portrait or most of the movie ads for the old Christmas movie, *Home Alone*. "Here in Tipton?"

"No. I think they rounded up the troublemakers around here back in 2013. Besides, that's not what I meant. Don't take this the wrong way since you and Fiona are buds, but the woman is hard to like."

"I know."

"She rubs people the wrong way."

"I know that, too."

"It wouldn't be too strange if someone took a dislike to her."

"That's possible. Even the employees at the shelter have a challenging time with the woman, despite the fact she took some of our most unadoptable dogs and put the shelter in her will, but that's supposed to be secret. The will part, I mean."

"Okay." She held up her index finger as she worked out the possible scenario. "People talk. Let's say a group of people Fiona offended got together and decided to play a trick on her. Maybe one pens her a note. Another calls, and a third sets a fire."

"Is there a fourth who kidnaps her?"

"No." Expecting people to take simple prank up to kidnapping ruined her scenario. "I'm not convinced Fiona has been kidnapped. Ransom notes or phone calls come with a kidnapping. All sorts of things could have happened, from Fiona going to another town to check out their shelter and getting detained, to having car problems. I'm still with the this is just a prank theory."

"Hmm." Karly tugged at her ear. "You went to your car to retrieve your weapon just because some insulted people were having fun at Fiona's expense?"

Max angled his head to address Nala. "Yeah, what's up with that?"

"I don't remember inviting you into this conversation."

Max backed away from the table and plopped down on the floor with his head on his front paws and his face arranged in a morose fashion.

"Nala, you upset him." Karly rushed over to the dog. As she petted him, she fussed over him. "Don't worry about it. She doesn't mean it. She's a little cranky because this case has her beat."

"The case does not have me beat. By the way, you're playing into Max's act. He's not morose, depressed, or anything like that. The dog just likes to get his way."

Karly continued to stroke Max, murmuring that it wasn't his fault, with the implication being somehow Nala had done something wrong. Nala placed her fork beside her plate, picked up her napkin, and wiped her face before she stood.

"I'm off to get my laptop. You and Max can continue to converse about what a horrible owner I am." She was at the door when Max padded up to her with a hopeful look in his brown eyes. He nudged her with his nose, his way of getting her attention.

"I assume I'm going."

It didn't take him long to get over his crestfallen state. Even though his play acting made her look bad, she still felt somewhat guilty about turning him down. "No. Officer Max is on duty. Your orders are to guard the house and Karly."

She expected some back talk or at least whining. Instead, he sat at attention, held his nose at what her mother called a regal angle and responded. "Yes, sir. Will comply."

Being addressed as sir bothered her a bit, but she didn't want to retrain her dog. It was obvious her father had his hand in this. She may not have provided a grandchild to allow her mother a chance to play glam ma, which was short for glamorous grandma, but she'd certainly pleased her father by bringing Max into the family.

"I'll expect a report when I return, Officer."

"Will do." He held up his hand and pawed at the air, still working on formulating a snappy salute.

"Forget about it."

He dropped the paw and stared at it as if it offended him somehow.

"I'll be back in a couple of hours."

Max gave a quick glance over his shoulder in the direction of the kitchen. "Please hurry. Karly thinks she's the Dr. Phil of dog psychologists. She'll be wanting to talk about feelings. Yuck!" He stuck out his tongue as if tasting something bad.

"I'll do my best. You'll be fine as long as you don't chat about Tyler Goodnight anymore."

"Hey, that was my go-to distractor. You use clowns. I have Tyler."

"You don't have Tyler," she reminded him as she opened the door, passed through the exit and closed it softly. She didn't have Tyler, either. What she did have was one confusing situation. Why couldn't people come to her with cut and dried scenarios? The idea made her wrinkle her nose at the ridiculousness of the thought. Easy to solve cases didn't need the help of a cut-rate investigator.

Chapter Twelve

THE VIEW FROM her rearview mirror was a gray plume of dust highlighted by her car lights. The dawn to dusk house lights flickered on with the approaching night, as did the security lights. A border collie ran the length of his yard and barked at her. Obviously, the owner had an invisible fence. Just as well, she didn't want to play a game of dodge dog with a pooch determined to herd Natalie, her car.

Her phone chimed as she approached the county road. "Hello."

"It's Elvin. I came up with a big goose egg."

"What do you mean?" The man she knew would never admit to failure.

"The sample you gave me was little more than lighter fluid and newspaper. Not much of a challenge for my associate."

Even though it was pretty much what she expected, it didn't provide the details that might scare up a suspect. If she'd hoped for an immediate hit on a known arsonist, then she was out of luck. "I thought that's what it was, which means—"

Before she could finish the sentence, Elvin interrupted. "It could be just about anyone, even Karly."

"Please, it's not Karly. She's possibly the only person who can tolerate the woman."

"Look at you, standing up for your friend. How sweet." His voice had turned soft and mocking.

"I'm not standing up for anyone. Stating a fact. I noticed you talking up Karly and even giving her the old granite profile."

"Jealous?"

"Not hardly."

"If not, why did you mention the profile? Only someone who was jealous would have noticed that. As for talking to Karly—especially if she's the culprit—let's just say I like my ladies a little twisted."

Nala made gagging noises. "Come on. Didn't we talk about this before? I need you to be professional in our association. I am not one of the guys."

"I've noticed. Several times, even."

"Elvin!"

"Okay, I'll stop. Getting back to your newspaper and lighter fluid, I'd say your harasser is an amateur or at best in a rush."

"Why?"

"Anyone has lighter fluid and newspaper."

"Do they? Gas grills have replaced charcoal grills. I hardly see charcoal lighter fluid for sale except in the summer months."

"My bad. I meant the fluid you use in cigarette and cigar lighters, not b-b-q. Those with fancy lighters refill theirs as opposed to tossing them like the cheap plastic lighters."

"That is something. Bloody the blood hound smelt cigarette smoke. This confirms that whoever started the fire is a smoker. Now I know the person had a fancy lighter, which probably means he's a hardcore smoker."

"This helps you how, and did I just hear you refer to getting information from a bloodhound?"

Oops, she hadn't meant to say that. Exhaustion was getting to her if she made a goof that large. "By knowing the person is a smoker, I eliminated about seventy-five percent of the population of Indiana. Someone who has a fancy lighter is probably an older male."

"Not necessarily. There are plenty of expensive cigar bars here in Indy. I've been to Nicky Blaine's Cocktail Lounge and Blend Bar and Cigar."

"I didn't know you smoked."

"You don't know everything about me. I like to try new things. Anyhow, you'd be surprised how many women smoke cigars, and those are the ones that do so in public."

"I thought we were talking about flashy lighters, not women and cigars."

"I'm getting there. Anyhow, cigars aren't cheap, so no one is going to pull out a cheap lighter and light one up. Most of the guys, even the millenials, have these expensive lighters. It's kind of like a James Bond thing. They're posers, of course, pretending to be all suave and debonair."

From the contempt apparent in his tone, it meant someone had outdone Elvin in the lighter department. "I guess old men are out as a culprit."

"Not necessarily, but who would want to hike that far. I know I wouldn't."

"Yeah, but whoever it was could have come up the drive, turned off their lights as he approached. Then when the alarms went off, he could either hide and watch or hightail it out of there."

"Did Karly and Fiona hear a vehicle leaving?"

She heaved a heavy sigh. As eyewitness accounts went, theirs were totally lacking. "They didn't mention it, but consider twenty dogs barking in alarm. I doubt they could hear anything at all."

It brought her back full circle except for a lighter. Anyone who needed an upscale lighter smoked a great deal, but she should have figured that out if he was smoking while committing a crime. The fact that the perpetrator smoked while setting a fire meant nerves of steel or a total amateur. Even criminals watched television and saw how perps were identified by their cigarette butts by the brand and the DNA left on the filter. Now, she wasn't totally sure if that was a do-able thing, but it was all over the crime shows, which meant those in the know would avoid it.

Right back where she was before, except in the morning she'd comb the grounds around the kennel, outside the fence, and along the road. Good chance whoever it was spent time waiting for what they considered the perfect moment. While he waited, he could have smoked and been careless enough to toss a spent butt. It was a stupid thing to do, but plenty of people did stuff out of habit without thought entering the matter. Elvin continued talking. "Dogs barking could be an issue. I imagine they went to check out the dogs before anything else."

"They put the fire out and then checked on the dogs."

"Then they called the police."

"Yes."

"Sorry I wasn't more help."

"Me, too. Maybe tomorrow I can find you a cigarette butt to analyze."

"Saliva tests don't come cheap."

"I expected as much." None of the tests she had Elvin run were inexpensive, except for the first one when she'd won in a bet. "I'll call you tomorrow."

"Good deal. Then you can explain your special skill that allows you to talk to the animals."

So much for changing the subject. "It's nothing. I just listen really. See ya." She hung up before Elvin could reply.

A lighter didn't feel like much of a clue, but it brought her one step closer than before. Maybe her father would call back about the handwriting soon. Normally, unless they had a sample on file, the analysis didn't tell her who had written the note.

Her mind played with various outcomes of the handwriting analysis as she made the appropriate turns to reach her office. By the time she arrived the sun had set, which made her miss Max. Memories of the homeless and the occasional drunk who appeared after dark worried her a little. Most were harmless, but assumed, as a female, she'd be good for a handout. It took a lot of cold shouldering and threats to call the police to get them to leave her alone after she made the initial mistake of giving one down on his luck fellow a couple of bucks.

Her office building used to be a thriving concern with an exclusive furniture store that consumed the entire bottom floor. Now, people, or at least the younger ones, headed out to Fishers where a new IKEA store recently opened. Her mother had been quite vocal about the furniture store, feeling it would have a direct impact on her business. Her father had reassured her that her customer base wanted things done for them while IKEA customers were content to assemble their own furniture.

The entrance to the building she usually used had the parking area zoned for loading and another half dozen handicapped parking places in front of it, which meant customers using the building couldn't even park reasonably close. So far, anyone who had found their way into her office hadn't called ahead for her to tell them where to park, and must have figured it out on their own.

The compact car festooned with several superhero logos and one bumper sticker that read *Using your turn signal is not giving information to the enemy* meant Harry was still here. The thought cheered her a little. Her hand went up to her hair, which was probably a mess.

"Why do you care?"

She questioned herself as if she were an alter ego. Her mother would insist a woman owed it to herself to look put together every minute of the day. Caring would imply she had a need to look her best for Harry. She didn't. They were friends, and on two occasions, coworkers, when she hired him to help tail someone. Max would have done a wonderful job, but people could be weird about allowing a dog in a shopping center, hotel, or restaurant, especially an unaccompanied one, which was why she had to hire Harry.

Nala parked her car behind Harry's. She exited the car and locked it, before strolling to the door using her *I mean business stride*, which was probably the equivalent of a banty rooster puffing up to look more intimidating. Her posture remained straight, utilizing her height with her heeled boots that made her probably five foot seven. In her defense class, the teacher had emphasized posture was everything. Muggers looked for women with rounded shoulders and a faltering walk, knowing such a person would not fight back.

Her phone chimed. The trio of notes meant her mother, but she'd have to wait. The same instructor informed her that answering your phone in a public setting put you at a disadvantage. Instead of paying attention to your surroundings, you interact with whomever you were talking to.

The phone stopped ringing as she jogged up the steps, but she knew her mother well enough to know she'd call back immediately. The meager building exterior light illuminated the stoop enough for her to pick out the right key. As she bent to insert it, a strip of cardboard sticking out near the bottom of the door caught her attention. It was a common practice for someone unloading multiple items to use the use cardboard or anything else that was handy to keep the door from locking. Harry probably did it and forgot to remove it.

As soon as she removed the cardboard, entered and locked the door from the inside, which was standard protocol, the phone started buzzing again. Feeling safe enough inside the lighted hallway with a locked door between her and the unknown, she reached for her phone and thumbed it on.

"Hello, Mother."

"It's about time you answered."

"I was driving." Which wasn't too far from the truth. Her father was a stickler about not talking on the cell while driving. Even though her mother had a fancy sedan that allowed her to talk hands free on the phone using her Bluetooth, she sometimes got in heated debates with vendors who failed to deliver furniture orders on time. Once, it caused her to rear-end someone. Ironically, it was someone she knew. They had a laugh about it, and her mother paid for the damages out of pocket. Because of this, Nala knew it was an acceptable excuse.

"Your father will be happy to know you aren't talking and driving."

Sometimes, her mother could wander off topic and spend ten minutes rambling on about something not pertinent to the reason she'd called. "I bet you didn't call to talk about driving and talking on the phone."

"You're right." Her mother gave a little, tinkling laugh. "I want to tell you about my newest hobby. Beverly introduced me to it."

Bev had been her mother's best friend for as long as Nala could remember. Since Bev tended to be on the quiet, conservative side, she could bet it wasn't drag racing or sky diving. "What's your new hobby?"

"I'm doing our family tree."

Of course she was. Since this tended to be a popular hobby with people her mother's age, she was surprised it hadn't been done already. At least it was better than her mother's former obsession with being a grandmother, which relied on her as the only child.

"That sounds great. What brought this on?"

"You know Beverly has traced her family back to 16th century Scotland. She has someone who served under Mary, Queen of Scots. She's also related to the poet, Robert Burns, and one of her great greats was a pirate, although Bev likes the term, privateer. I figure we must have just as many interesting characters in our family tree. Maybe not so much on your father's side, but on mine."

Oh, it sounded like a competition to her, which was something her mother excelled at. If Bev could come up with a colorful family tree, then her mother's would be a rainbow tree, even if she had to invent a few great greats.

"Sounds like fun. Are you doing this online with one of those companies or something?"

Nala held the phone to her ear as she walked up the first set of stairs. Normally, she wasn't at the office this late at night. Even though she'd chosen the office based on the price, she hadn't considered how creepy it would be at night with all its assorted creaks, echoes, and shadows where the lights didn't reach.

"Those companies are for beginners. Bev and I go down to the State Library where they have a genealogy section devoted to it with special assistants. So far, I've traced my family back to before the state was formed in 1816. Outside of a great grand who may have run a saloon in Cincinnati, I've found nothing. I had high hopes of finding something in the past since apparently our family line ends with you."

Whoa, here she hoped the family tree would bypass the need for her to reproduce. "Find any missing relatives or anything?"

A stream of light came from Harry's office. He ran some type of clearing house for collectibles, mainly comic book characters and such. If someone notified him about the need for something, he could locate it for a price if he didn't already have it. Odd, that he was here so late, but Halloween was creeping up, and many of his customers would want the perfect costume as opposed to a cheap knock off. She made a mental note to say hello on her way back down. She continued to the third flight of stairs that led to her office smack in the middle of nothing. No one had rented the offices on either side of her, which wasn't too peculiar since the building itself was in a forgotten part of the Circle City. Besides being cheap, Nala chose it because people wouldn't have to worry about bumping into their neighbors or co-workers as they visited to secure her services.

Her mother chattered on about a cousin she located in Provo, Utah and another one in Boca Raton, Florida. "I'm shocked at how accurate the information is. When Glenda married that serviceman who took her off to Europe, I figured that was it. Imagine my surprise to see Glenda's name and address in the files. Most of it is online, but you can find a great deal by just looking. It might even be useful to you if you had to look someone up. Maybe some guy could be passing himself off as being related to the royal family, and all you'd need to do is come to the library and look it up."

"Who's Glenda?"

"My cousin, which would make her your cousin, too."

True. Her mother had uncovered a slew of relatives, which

meant she might be able to do the same for Fiona. The library could be useful, plus it was free. Besides, it wouldn't make her suffer through a bunch of sexist comments before delivering info. Although to be honest, Elvin was better than he had been. That may not be saying much, but she had to give him some credit for trying.

Her mother bemoaned the lack of colorful relatives at this point. "Mom, maybe you just need to go back further. There's a good chance we have at least a witch or a serial killer in the ranks."

"You're so right, dear. I'm giving up too soon. We could be related to Jack the Ripper and the royal family since most people think Jack was the Prince of Wales."

"You better go check that out."

"I will. No time to chat. I have research to do. Love you."

"Love you, too." Her mother had already hung up without hearing her comment. Nala shook her head in amusement. Only her mother would be thrilled to have a serial killer in the family tree. Would a murderer beat a blood thirsty pirate? She hoped for her sake it would because it would keep her mother from obsessing about her lack of grandchildren.

Her goal was to get her computer and bullets, and say hey to Harry on her way out. Though he usually had a solid habit of leaving by five, the man was probably overwhelmed trying to get out Wonder Woman and Batman costumes to true fans. Ones willing to pay much more for an outfit than those buying theirs at the local discount store.

Nala smiled at the painted letters on her door, *Nala Bonne, Private Investigator, Discreet Inquiries.* Originally, she intended to use stick-on letters, but her mother practically had a meltdown when she heard about it. Somehow, she thought it was a reflection on her interior design business. The next day Nala arrived to find gold cursive lettering on her door. Knowing her mother, it was probably gold leaf. All she could do was thank her mother, even though she had wanted to do it herself.

Her school friends thought it must be grand to be an only child. Maybe it was in some ways, but she ended up being the one who had to juggle the hopes and dreams her parents had for her. Different personalities wanted different things. In the end, she had to abandon their wants and desires for her own.

After finding the right key, bearing a little bit of red fingernail polish to help her remember, she placed her left hand on the door to hold it steady, but it swung open under her hand.

The street light streamed in through the open blinds, making skinny rectangles of light on the floor. The door was unlocked when it shouldn't have been. Hadn't she locked it? Could be she'd forgotten, trying to herd Max out. Her first thought was to call someone so she didn't enter the ominously unlocked office alone. Would another investigator do that? No experienced veteran would. One of her goals was to prove to her father that she had the cojones to do the job. Technically, she didn't, but it was just an expression, implying boldness and courage.

At least if she made some noise Harry would know she was there. Nala drifted back to the stairs and stomped up and down the last six steps leading to the landing several times. If anyone was in her office that should give him time to leave. The downside is he'd have to go past her since only a super hero would be capable of crawling down the exterior of the building.

She slammed her open door a few times, then talked in a forced deep voice.

"I don't know when Nala Bonne will be here, but I need to talk to her."

Feeling as if she needed another person, she modified her male voice to have a Southern accent. "Well, now y'all have to wait until the renowned investigator returns."

She wasn't too sure if her fake customers should say anything more. All she had to do was push the door open and turn on the light switch. Unfortunately, the switch was about four feet from the door making it awkward to reach. Using the toe of her shoe, she pushed the door open wider and ran in, hunched over just in case someone might make a grab for her. Once the light was on, she pushed back against the wall, surveying the room.

The orange crushed velvet couch with black dog hair was still there, along with the Oriental rug and slipper chair her mother had gifted her. Not that any robber would have taken off with those items since they would be difficult to move. She'd better check her closet to see if her ammo and laptop were still there. The closed door to the inner office beckoned her, but it was a call that could wait until another day. Get the laptop, the bullets, and leave.

Fortunately, she had a light in the closet that helped immensely. It didn't help height wise. She had to balance on her tippy toes to reach for the bullets, which meant she put them up there when she still had her mother's stepladder. Nala was blindly reaching for the bullets when a voice called out.

"What are you doing?"

She whirled around knocking over the box of ammo and littering the floor with bullets. Her eyes went to the closed inner door only to find it shut. Harry stepped in the room from the hall and grinned at her.

"Oh, it's you. I thought I heard someone in your office. I wasn't sure someone wasn't breaking into your office, considering the creepy water guy."

Her heart that had shot into overdrive, gradually slowed down. Nala spoke as she knelt to pick up the dropped bullets. "Oh, that noise." She flushed but forced herself to continue. "It was me. When I came up the stairs, I saw your light on and figured there must be a super hero costume rush for Halloween."

"You got that right. Everyone wants to be Wonder Woman and not the traditional costume, which would be easy enough to get, but they want the new movie Wonder Woman version. I had stockpiled fifty in anticipation of this, but they're gone. I'm spending most of my time emailing potential customers back with alternative suggestions."

"That explains why you're still here."

Harry stooped to pick up a bullet that was near his feet. "Should I ask why you need bullets, or is that on a need to know basis like your stomping?"

Nala rocked back on her heels with her fingers cupped around the gathered bullets. Indecision gripped her as she pondered what to tell Harry. He'd always been a help since the first day she took the office. His sincere eyes behind his trendy glasses, ready smile, and well-trimmed beard made her think of a teddy bear. If not a bear, then a dog that was eager to please. There was nothing to fear. Unlike most men, Harry was honest and uncomplicated. What she saw was what she got.

She lurched to a standing position and moved to her dropped purse. She held up her cupped hands. "These, as you can guess, are for my gun. I emptied my gun when I practiced with my father. I forgot to reload it. It's hard to be intimidating with an empty gun."

"It's possible." Harry skirted around her and reached the ammo box. He snatched the carton and held it under her hands. "Go ahead and put them in the box. It must be better than carrying them in your purse. You could reach in for lipstick and pull out a bullet."

The bullets tinged bouncing off one another as they tumbled into the box. Harry retrieving the box for her summed up the man. He identified a problem and solved it.

"Thanks. I appreciate your help. When I got up to the office the door was unlocked, which isn't like me. It's not that I have a lot to steal, but I lock it to keep files confidential. That's the real reason I made so much noise. I wanted you to know I'd been here just in case I vanished or something."

"There are better ways." He arched one eyebrow. "Did you think of knocking on my door?"

All the stomping and running up and down the stairs seemed so silly now. "I was going to before I left to say hi on my way out, but that was before I discovered the unlocked door. I'm extremely tired, which probably taxes my deductive skills."

"Hear ya. I need to get going, too. Grab what you need and meet me at my office. I'll head down and lock up. There are only so many wannabe superheroes I can disappoint in a day. See ya soon." He held up his hand in acknowledgement.

"Will do." The possibility of walking out together had Nala shoving the bullet box in her oversized purse and reaching for her laptop. She gave the closed inner door one final look before leaving. The sound of Harry's hurried steps echoed in the stairwell. If she just left the light on, she could catch up with him. It had nothing to do with the half dozen steps she'd have to make in the dark before she reached the door.

She twisted the lock on the door and pulled it shut. A firm shake proved the door was well and truly locked. Her eyes stayed on the doorknob as if it might turn into a snake and bite her. A deadbolt would make a lot more sense, especially considering the neighborhood. That would go on her to-do when she had the funds list.

Harry stood near the landing with his backpack on one shoulder and his dark office behind him. The sight of him waiting, so dependable, caused a rush of affection.

"Hey, there," he called out. "You live around here?"

"No." She shrugged her shoulders. "You?"

"Far enough away I don't hear sirens every ten minutes. I'm surprised I stayed so long with the total weirdness of the day."

They fell in step descending the stairs. Nala was willing to bet her day could beat his for being totally off the wall, but she should hear him out before making a snap decision. "What was so weird about your day?"

"Went to Starbucks to get coffee as usual."

"Yeah," she encouraged him to continue, truly hoping he had something better than that.

"Since I go to the same shop and walk in at the same time, my coffee is usually waiting."

"Un-huh." Nothing different so far.

They reached the ground floor, and Harry held open the heavy exterior door for her as he continued talking. "When I went to pay, I was told an admirer had already paid for me."

"That's different. Do you know who it was?"

He grimaced. "That's where it gets weird. The barista angled his head to the right where several people were sitting, drinking their coffee. There was this attractive Asian girl sitting by herself. I was hoping it was her, but outside the store window was a clown waving at me. I left immediately."

"You think you have a clown admirer?"

"I don't know. It could be the season." He paused. "Every year around this time the clown sightings start."

"It's more likely your admirer is an employee. Someone who sees you every day and knows your habits." It felt obvious to her. Otherwise, some woman would have to shadow Harry to discover his movements, which spelled obsession as opposed to attraction.

"Thanks for putting that into perspective. It might be some campaign the store is running or something to make customers happy."

"If so, it must be an expensive one. Can't you accept that someone might have a crush on you? Women are getting more assertive nowadays and aren't waiting around for men to do the asking."

"Are you referring to yourself?"

They walked down the front steps slowly and hung a left. Every other streetlight was out, which made her wonder if it was an energy saving effort as opposed to being burnt out. Whatever it was added to the eerie atmosphere. She wished Max were with her, but Harry would have to fill in for him.

"You didn't answer me," her companion prompted.

Obviously, he'd asked her something, but she'd been distracted by the streetlights. Unwilling to ask and seem like a total flake, she decided to go with the ambiguous answer. "I could be."

"Hmm." Harry held up his keys and pushed his fob as they drew closer to their cars. It made Nala wish for a second that she had the luxury of a fob. "I'm headed out to Bru Burger for a bite. Would you be interested? I could tell you about the creepy water guy and continue the totally weird day."

"It does sound tempting, but Max and Karly are waiting on me. Can you give me the condensed version of creepy water guy?"

Harry shoved his hands in his pockets and peered down at his feet for a moment, before looking back up. "Not a lot to tell. Dude in a water shirt follows me in. Tells me he's here to pick up water bottles. I told him there were some in the basement. He headed down there."

She held up one finger. "Am I missing something?"

Harry met her eyes and gave a solemn nod. "I don't use a water service. I suspect you don't."

"You're right."

"Today, I actually saw Delores and her little dog. She's the only full-time resident I know who lives in the building. I asked her if she used the water service. She said she never did, but mentioned a lawyer who once had an office who could have used one. Only he's been gone for at least three years."

"That's odd. Did you see the creepy water guy leave?"

"No. I went to my office and didn't even give the man a second thought until I talked to Delores. After that, I remembered I asked him why he wasn't bringing replacement water in and he told me the account had been cancelled. There was no water truck idling in the loading area when I entered the building."

The man could be in the building still. She wasn't sure why someone would want to be in the building. The best she could do was notify the super who would probably do nothing. Maybe she should have opened the inner office door. She shuddered, but covered it by chafing her arms.

"You need to get in your car. Forgive me for rambling on about the bogus water guy."

"What makes you think he was bogus?"

"A feeling and he was too clean and pressed."

"Being neat is suspicious now."

"You know what I mean. A guy who is hauling stuff around all day won't make an effort to press his pants."

"He could be new." Nala hoped to reassure herself more than

Harry.

"Shows up where no one has a water service and without a truck."

"Sounds odd. I'll call the super."

"Could you not mention I let him in?"

"You got it." Nala circled the front of her car to reach the driver side. Despite having pushed his fob, Harry waited on the curb, which perplexed her until she realized he was being a gentleman. The man had class. She gave a spritely honk to acknowledge his actions as she drove off.

TOBY'S LITTLE FORAY into the basement wasn't exactly helpful. The furniture from Gabe and his office were shoved into the storage area corner along with the carpet and the stupid basset hound doorstop. His partner had bought it claiming it was art and would give the place a bit more of a high brow atmosphere.

He rattled the change in his pocket as his eyes searched the sidewalk for his would-be helper. Zed, a homeless man who had the look of a lumberjack, agreed to meet him after his meal at the shelter. Tonight was meatloaf night, and Zed refused to miss it.

Toby congratulated himself on not living in a shelter. If he were honest with himself, he wasn't far from it. If he had a truck, he could take the office furniture. Technically it was half his, but people moving furniture in the middle of the night tended to attract unwanted attention.

The sound of voices meant someone was coming. He stepped back into the shadows, wondering for a brief moment if Zed had brought a friend who might also want to earn a twenty. The hipster guy, who so conveniently let him in that morning, exited along with that girl detective. They were chatting away. The stupid woman had no clue he'd been in her office.

Her office didn't have much he could fence. Besides, he only wanted what was owed to him, which would be the emeralds. They hadn't made an appearance in their original form or separated in the jewel world. The main stone was huge and would have been remembered. It was starting to look as if his partner really did die in a car crash as rumored. It would serve him right and would mean the jewels were out there. Gabe probably stowed them somewhere he considered clever while waiting for the right buyer. He wouldn't have had any issues with double crossing the original client, especially considering Toby was nabbed for the crime.

The tall form of a man came around the corner. Zed. Right on time, too, a little better than he expected from a homeless dude. He jogged across the street, darting around a lone taxi. He waved to get the man's attention.

"Hey, Zed! So glad you're here. This should only take a minute."

The bearded giant gave him a nod. "Good deal. I'd like to get back in time for the movie. I think it is one of those inspirational things. Still, a movie is a movie. All you want me to do is help you move some furniture? Nothing illegal, right? I made a clean start of things. Walking the straight and narrow."

"No funny stuff." Toby sucked in his lips, preventing a snide comment about how the straight and narrow had Zed living in a shelter. Reformed cons could be as big a pain as former smokers. Right now, Zed was all he had to work with, which meant he had to make the story believable. "My former business partner and I moved in together. He's gone now, and I want to change where I have my desk. Want to move it closer to the window."

He was about to elaborate, but he stopped himself. Liars always gave themselves away by giving too many details. What he really needed was to get to the secret hidey hole that Gabe had created in the office floor. It happened to be underneath the huge desk. It was the next possible hiding place for the emeralds.

"Okay. Let's do it."

Toby gestured to the building and raced ahead of Zed to open the door. He'd carefully placed a piece of cardboard he'd duct-taped into the exterior door frame to keep it from locking. The third-floor office door could be opened by rattling the knob vigorously. Fortunately, girl detective hadn't replaced the loose lock yet. He couldn't guarantee how long that would last.

He placed his hand on the doorknob and tugged. It didn't budge. It must be stuck. He jiggled it without luck. Zed came up behind him.

"You forget your key?"

Toby forced a laugh. "Yeah, something like that." He wasn't sure who decided to remove his impromptu cardboard passkey, but someone did.

Zed held up his hands. "Hey, man, I told you nothing illegal."

Toby ground his back molars together as he stared at his hand on the door handle. He'd have to try another time and try a different scheme to get in. He wouldn't be able to depend on Mr. Punctual who let him in earlier. The best way to stay out of jail was to blend in. Showing up again for a non-existent water service would not work twice.

Whenever he managed to get in, he'd still need muscle to wrestle the desk from its current spot. "Tell you what," he pivoted, expecting to give Zed a fiver and a promise to return, but the man had fled.

Toby closed his eyes briefly, then cursed as he trotted down the stairs. It wouldn't be good to be seen on the steps, especially if the girl detective figured out her door had been picked. He had locked it on his way out, hadn't he? A good thief always left the scene the same way he'd found it, minus the goodies. That way it takes longer for the rich folks to realize they'd been burgled. Some might even think they'd misplaced the item. In the end, they had insurance to replace whatever was stolen.

Chapter Thirteen

THE DRIVE BACK to Fiona's compound gave her time to think. An announcement on the radio asked people not to dress themselves or their children up as clowns this Halloween. The disc jockey of the hour fanned the issue by asking listeners to phone in if they thought it was their constitutional right to don a big red nose. Many called in and stated after they'd been told not to dress up like a clown, they would.

Harry may have had a weird day, but she was almost sure hers wore oversized shoes and a rainbow wig. Fiona might even be back home with some believable tale about why she was unreachable for most of the day. There were stretches on 65 where cellphone service blinked out. She could be there for some reason or her phone was dead, stolen, or lost. Still, it didn't explain why the woman hadn't driven home when she realized she was without a phone.

The ditch flew by, along with the dairy, and the showcase neighbors who had their lights on. She crept up the gravel drive not wanting to fling a stone at Natalie's delicate undercarriage. Vintage cars had charm, but when something needed to be replaced it was either astronomical due to lack of available parts or had to be machined, which was also expensive.

All the lights were on at the house, making it a contender for most excessive use of lights in Tipton County. Nala honked the horn at the closed gate, but not in a playful manner as before. Her inability to find a quick answer to Fiona's disappearance worried her. When she got inside the house, she'd call her father. It would help to have every officer cruising to be on the lookout for the missing car. Right now, all she was doing was sitting tight and hoping Fiona would come back, which wasn't enough.

Max darted out of the house and ran to the gate barking as Karly followed much slower. She walked toward the fence, but stopped to fuss with a small box on a post. The gates swung open as soon as she typed the code into it. A control box outside, too? How easy would it be for someone to reach the controls? It wasn't close. Someone would have to have twelve-foot arms or a device that would allow them to reach that far. Then there would be the issue of knowing the code. If Nala didn't trust her friend, Karly would be the perfect suspect. Any other person would suspect her. She had the motive and the ability to enter the place with ease.

The thought teased her as she drove in, making her doubt herself. Part of the reason she chose to go into investigation was she always had a gut feeling. It was a little fluttery sensation as opposed to a voice. It didn't mean she always listened to it. Jeff served as her perfect example of failing to heed her internal alarm system.

Still, she'd known Karly for years and knew the woman wasn't motivated by money. The shelter wasn't paying her enough to allow her to move into a house of her own. Even the rent on a modest one was more than her friend could afford.

Instead of a little devil on her shoulder, she had a tiny Sherlock Holmes that insisted on examining every angle. Could be that Karly was tired of struggling to get by. Who wouldn't be? The idea of maintaining a Fiona's smaller kennel and getting paid for it would be right down her alley. She wouldn't have to deal with the public, and it would free up a lot of time. Maybe she could go back to school or pick up a hobby. Then again, she'd worry about those at the shelter that didn't get adopted or the strays that didn't get found.

Nala parked the car and turned off the engine, but her mind continued to race, coming up with uncomfortable scenarios. The car door swung open, surprising her. Karly shot her a quizzical look.

"What's got your brow so furrowed? What are you thinking so hard about?"

Nothing she wanted to admit to. She glanced down at her hands, trying to compose her face. Her father used to joke that she'd never be a good poker player the way her emotions usually played across her face like a movie for everyone to see. However, teaching had helped, especially with children sharing details about Daddy sleeping on the couch or Mother having trouble walking straight. Even though she knew some of the parents' more interesting habits, she managed to hold a straight face at parent pick up.

Nala snagged her purse, but had to grab the laptop before exiting the car. "Have you heard from Fiona?"

"No." She rubbed her hands one over the other, betraying her feelings on that matter. "I'm worried, too."

By this time, Nala suspected something had happened. Even though she played the devil's advocate and considered the rescue dog queen wasn't exactly great with time. Things like that didn't matter when you worked from home. Would the dogs guilt her for being late? Max would, but that was an entirely different story. As if sensing her thoughts, Max leisurely picked his way across the drive.

"Did you bring me anything? Maybe…" he stretched the word out and managed to lift his doggy brows, "…a cheeseburger?"

"No. I didn't. I went to the office. As you well know is not the repository of cheeseburgers."

"Aw." His head went down, and his shoulders slumped forward, the image of dejection. "I hoped to get a little treat considering how hard I'm working on this case." He sat, cocked his head, warming up to his subject. "You think I enjoy talking to those kennel hounds? They aren't exactly sparkling conversationalists. They have one track minds, usually food, and if that isn't enough, they whine about it."

Really? He didn't see any similarities? "Remind you of anyone?"

Max moved his jaw back and forth as he concentrated almost as if he were chewing. It probably related to her father saying he'd chew on something when he meant mulling it over. Finally, he looked up at her. "Barney, the golden retriever down the street."

Her phone chimed, delaying her attempt to connect Max with reality. Luckily, she had remembered to turn the ringer on and placed it on top of the bullet box for easier access.

"Hello."

"It's me, Dad."

"I know. You have your own ringtone. Dragnet."

"Fitting."

Karly was motioning to her, holding her hand up to her ear as if a phone. She handed the phone to her friend.

"Captain Bonne. Okay, Spencer. It feels weird calling you that. Have you heard anything about Fiona?"

Whatever her father said didn't please her.

"She doesn't have anyone else to file a missing person's report. I'm it. Yeah, I know the car. She was driving a white Ford Fusion with a vanity plate that reads Dogs28. I'm not sure what the 28 was for, unless 27 other people wanted a plate that read dogs…Thanks."

She handed the phone back to Nala who held it up to her ear. "Dad?" Nothing, she looked at her cell and realized the call had ended.

"Oh, yeah. Your father told me to tell you he'd call you back. He wanted to get the missing person thing going. He told me they could have taken my report earlier, but they're a little leery of running people down that are only a little late. There's an APB on the car now."

"You can count on him. Sometimes people declare a spouse is missing when they know their spouse is with someone else and want the police to burst in on them. It's surprising the police have time to get anything done with so many people calling in bogus stuff."

"Yeah. It's good your father is a cop."

"Most of the time. It made dating challenging if you can remember."

They both chuckled as Karly led the way into the house. "Yeah, most of the boys were afraid your father might trail them in a squad car or show up wherever you were."

"He did do that."

"Oh, yeah, I forgot."

Nala set the laptop on the table and booted it up. "Can I assume that Fiona has Internet?"

"She does. The password is Dogs28."

"Dogs28 again." She typed in the password as Karly turned to close the door after Max.

The idea she had earlier when talking to her mother returned. Using the search engine, she found the library genealogy easy enough. She typed in Fiona Bridgewater and found, surprisingly, that there were two. One married a Bridgewater while another was born a Bridgewater. Yeah, that's the one she wanted.

A chair scraped across the linoleum as Karly took a seat. "Are you working on the police sketch program you told me about?"

"Not yet. First, I decided to look at Fiona's family tree. Mom was bragging about the genealogy department at the library without realizing she could do it all from home. Told me it went back to the seventeenth century. Although, I don't need to go back that far."

Karly placed her elbow on the table and cupped her chin with her hand. "I already told you she has no family."

"I know. Still, people sometimes say that, and it just means they don't care for them."

"Do you think she went and stayed with one of them?"

Nala looked up from the computer. "Why would she do that?"

"You're the one looking for relatives." She shrugged her shoulders. "I figured you could tell me."

Unlike Nala, Karly had come from a large, boisterous family. The way the siblings good naturedly teased each other made Nala want a sister or brother. It would be hard for her friend to imagine your own relatives could be your worst enemies. If she needed any convincing, then all she'd have to do is read a police report or watch a daytime soap.

"I don't have much to go on. Even if we could just talk to a relative, we may find out a bit more about Fiona. How much do you really know about her?"

"Not much. I know she loves dogs and hates writing greeting cards."

"Why does she do it? Didn't she inherit boatloads of money?" Apparently, even Elvin had heard about it, which meant it had to be a known fact.

"I'm not sure about that. She did tell me the kennel cost much more than she expected, and she'd have to keep working her crappy job to keep them in kibble. Fiona even showed me some of the cards she did. They're the good ones, too, with the long sentimental poems."

"That's hard to believe." She turned back to the computer, typed in Fiona's name and date of birth. A file came up on the screen. "Do you know if her parents were Walter and Marilyn?"

"Parents' names weren't needed on the application to adopt," she told her and went to the kitchen.

"Okay. The birth certificate lists Marilyn and Walter as her parents. We know she has no siblings, but she could have aunts, uncles, and cousins out the wazoo."

Might as well start with the father. Nala typed in Walter Bridgewater and waited to see what she might get. A half dozen entries popped up. Wouldn't have thought the name was that popular. The first entry was a marriage document for Walter and a Greta Stamm that had taken place in Frankfurt, Germany. No, that couldn't be the right Walter. She checked the birthdate. That was the same. She did a little investigating and found a young Walter Bridgewater had joined the Army and had been stationed in Germany. It made her wonder what happened to Greta. A few more clicks uncovered a small newspaper announcement in German. Great, now she'd have to use the translator to read it and possibly type the whole thing in because it was a picture of a newspaper as opposed to a document.

This was investigative work at its most basic. She painstakingly typed in the German words into the translator, having some issues with the symbols. Not all the words translated, but she could understand enough that Walter and Greta Stamm welcomed a son, Herman Hugo Stamm.

"Did you know Fiona had a half-brother in Germany?"

"Seriously?" she called from the kitchen. "I'm still amazed she picked me to be her power of attorney. I'm keeping track of everything we're using so Fiona won't think we're taking advantage of her."

"Business expenses. She should expect a few. I found some cousins, too, Maureen and Debbie. I'll write down their names, and we might be able to find out more on social media."

"What good will that do us? I'm not sure how their vacation photos or political rants will help us." Karly strolled back to the table to peer at the information.

"I just need to know where they live. It could be Fiona stays in contact with them."

Max placed his head on the table. "I can't see anything."

"I'm not sure if dogs can read computer screens, despite the cute memes with dogs at computers."

His nose quivered as he sniffed. "Smells like you and the corned beef sandwich you ate last week. Not sure how you can find anyone using this box that takes up all your time."

"Records. They're all in here." She pointed to the screen. "It gives me information to start searching."

Max kept staring at the laptop. "You get information from this thing?"

"I do."

"Can you order food from it? Like the drive-thru. Just yell into it?"

They were back to that. She now fully understood the expression like a dog with a bone. "Even if I could order something, no one would deliver this far out."

By moving back to the kitchen, Karly interrupted the conversation that wasn't going anywhere. Max abandoned his inquiry to trail after a better prospect.

The familiar Dragnet television theme song played. Nala picked up her phone. "Hello, Dad."

"Got the boys looking for the car. I called back to discuss the handwriting. I scanned the note into the machine. Here's what I got.

The handwriting slants to the left and tends to go downhill, which indicates someone who's not outgoing, tends to be cynical or pessimistic. The writer keeps the dot on the I very close."

"What does that mean?"

"Stingy. Doesn't share. An individual who holds on tight to what he has and is probably jealous of others. Won't even give the dot a bit of air. The writer also uses a long slashing mark on the Ts, which shows a certain amount of arrogance and a desire to be in charge."

"That's a lot for a few marks possibly written in haste."

"Yeah, that's the best type of sample. One that is written without any knowledge that it might be analyzed."

"Does the analysis tell if it were a man or woman? Tall or short? Young or old?"

He gave a light chuckle. "Next you'll be asking me for an address. I've decided the author was male, not the analysis."

"Why is that?"

"Simple. Most women make some effort to write neatly or uniformly, whereas it seems men take pride in writing as badly as they can. This writer didn't even string his letters together even though they were obviously cursive, which means the person doesn't always think things out, which I also could have deduced from the note."

"Did they dust it for fingerprints?"

"They did and found three pairs, but none were in the data base. I suspect at least one set belongs to Fiona. Another set could be Karly's. If she comes in and gets fingerprinted we can eliminate her if this becomes a full-blown investigation. What're your thoughts on the matter?"

Indy's Finest in the mix would be an immense help, but it made things tricky for billing purposes. How much could she legitimately claim to have done on her own? Still, they had resources she didn't, such as the handwriting analysis. It hadn't told her that much though, other than the writer could be a cynical male who begrudged the dot over the eye a bit of space. The male part was questionable. She knew plenty of women who scribbled. The note author wasn't a people person, which should have made him understand Fiona's mindset. Obviously, not a dog person either, or maybe that part was a ruse. Often a perp would give what they thought was an acceptable motivation because the real reason could have been stupid and impulsive. Anything from someone taking the right of way to wearing the wrong team jersey had caused documented assaults. Her psychology classes hadn't been a total waste.

"At this point, I'm not sure if the note and disappearance are connected. We're going on the assumption they are until we find out otherwise. I'm using the library's genealogy files Mom told me about to discover any living relatives."

"Good call. Your mother will take credit if you come up with something useful."

"She can, especially since she was the one who brought up the family tree stuff while not so subtly hinting she had to go into the past since there wouldn't be any future Bonne offspring."

A hoarse chuckle came through the phone, making it feel as if her father were sitting right beside her.

"Princess, you don't go stressing over that. The way I see it is you have more than enough on your plate to do. If you happen to meet an upstanding citizen, with a good career and excellent credit, then I'd be happy for you."

"Thanks, Dad."

She hadn't missed he included a good credit score in his requirements. Her father had recently become convinced that anyone with a bad credit score would be open to bribes and payoffs.

"So, what are your plans?"

"Karly is staying here to wait for any news of Fiona and take care of the dogs. I'm going to keep her company since the idea of her being out in the country alone makes me nervous."

His father made the appropriate listening sounds, which meant he may or may not be listening. She'd witnessed several times how he appeared to pay attention when her mother was going on about a type of fabric or a couch style. Just to be sure, she thought she'd insert a check. "Max told me Fiona hasn't been here since the morning. He also did not find the smell of a stranger on the property."

"Interesting. That means she must have been taken elsewhere if she has truly been kidnapped."

What just happened? She told her father what they were doing, but when she mentioned Max it was like it was a done deal. Never mind the part about talking to a dog. "Ah, Dad, why do you suddenly believe Max's nose as opposed to everything I just said?"

"It's not that I don't believe you, princess."

He was calling her princess again, which made her feel all of five. It made her opinion little more than pink tulle and glitter, basically airy and shiny, with no concrete value. "Don't call me princess."

"Okay, aw..." Her father stalled as he stumbled for a name. "Nala, you told me what you're doing and going to do. Max not smelling an intruder is a fact. Dogs make good officers since they deal in facts as opposed to emotions. Even I have had preconceptions color the way I see something. I'm just saying dogs are facts only with no hidden agendas."

"I get that." Should she let her father try a little harder to dig himself out of the hole? As for being a fact-based animal, she glanced over at Max who was wobbling a little as he maintained the beg position for a treat. If you asked her, Max ran on emotions and hunger.

A phone burbled in the distance. Since she was on the phone, it couldn't be hers. It had that old-timey ring often associated with rotary phones on older television shows. She waved to get her friend's attention, thinking it was her phone. Karly had downloaded barking dogs as her ringtones and assigned Nala the frenzied barking of a chihuahua, which she totally nixed. Luckily, she changed it to a full-bodied shepherd bark, when she took Max.

"Excuse me," she murmured into the phone, then muted it. "Karly, the phone."

"Uh?" Her friend blinked and dropped her hand that clutched a dog treat she was ready to throw. "What?"

"Your phone is ringing."

"That's not my phone."

Max took advantage of the woman's distraction and pulled the treat from her hand.

"It's not mine."

They both realized the obvious at the same time. "It's Fiona's."

Nala scoured the kitchen for a wall phone without luck while Karly darted for the hall. If someone did kidnap Fiona, wouldn't they call the house to deliver ransom demands? She bolted into the hallway only to find her Karly holding the vintage rotary phone. No wonder she didn't have a answering machine.

"Who was it?"

"Whoever it was hung up."

"Call star 69. It should call them right back."

"What should I say?"

"Just ask them if they called this number. They should know. It might just be one of those windows people cold calling. In that case, tell them you are not the homeowner."

Nala held her cell to her chest, inhaled, and held her breath as her friend punched in the code, then listened. Whatever she heard caused her to wrinkle her nose.

"Bad news. It was either a blocked or private number. It could have been Fiona's kidnapper."

"Maybe. It could also be someone calling you from Florida to inform whoever answered the phone that she'd won a three-day resort giveaway, too."

Nala thumbed the mute off her phone and put it up to her ear. "Someone called and hung up. Karly tried to call them back, but it was a blocked number. Anyway, you get phone records?"

Her father cleared his throat first. "Not in a speedy manner, all the same it would show a blocked number. What you can do is call star 57, which basically has the ability to grab the call at that time. There's usually a fee, and the police must be informed."

"You already know. If Karly already called 69, can you still do this?"

"Not now, but if the phone rings again, you can."

"Thanks. This is valuable information. Does it work on cell phones?"

"No, but I can send you a link that tells you how to do something similar on a cell."

The cell vibrated and a blinking light informed her she had a message. Weird how tech-savvy her father was. "Got it."

"Good. Remember if anything is a little bit off, call me."

"I will."

"Don't wait until you're speeding down the road at high speed with gunmen shooting at you."

"That was only one case. Most aren't like that."

"Maybe, but it took ten years off my life. Luckily, your chatty friend, Elvin, never revealed to your mother the details of what happened that day."

"Yeah. That was fortunate." And so unlike Elvin who had no issue revealing all he knew if it would serve as a conversational tidbit. Her previous case had brought her parents in contact with Elvin, and somehow, he'd ingratiated himself. It didn't take much for her mother. All a person had to do was listen to her stories and compliment her on her wit, home, yard, business acumen, and her stylish appearance. She preferred remarks that implied she and Nala could be sisters.

Her father was a harder sell. It was easy enough to do background checks, but her father prided himself on his ability to read people. All the movie quotes and pretensions to be a player fell away when Elvin talked with her father. She wanted to tell him if he could be more like that with women, they wouldn't avoid him. Most of his dates consisted of women who saw him as a meal ticket or gullible enough to be used to make their boyfriends jealous.

When she contemplated being an investigator, she did some dry runs with her friends, only because she could confirm her findings. Most wouldn't come right out and agree she'd uncovered some details they'd rather have left unknown, but their expressions did. It made her feel like a peeping tom, but she had to start somewhere. Her most abundant source of information was social media.

"Um, Dad, I need to get off the phone and be ready if someone calls again."

"Understand. Keep me in the loop."

"Copy that." She thumbed off the phone with a smile. Every now and then Nala wanted her father to know she did remember some of the things he taught her. She might never talk on a police radio, but she could if she needed to.

Chapter Fourteen

Barking in the distance interrupted Nala's dream right when the Mediterranean hottie named Georgio held out his hand and invited her onto his sailboat. Something poked into her cheek. With a roll of her head, an electronic chirp sounded right in her ear and brought her head up in a snap. *Brownies*, she'd fallen asleep on her laptop keyboard.

An open document on the screen held the names of Fiona's cousins, Maureen and Debbie. Both lived in Texas with Maureen in San Antonio and Debbie in Austin. Under Maureen's name she'd typed married thirty years to Jason Plough, two children, a granddaughter, and a dog named Trixie.

Under Debbie's name was divorced, no children, angry that her husband of twenty-two years left her for a much younger woman. It was all starting to come back. It was obvious the sisters stayed in contact due their comments and consistent likes of each other's posts. While most people agreed with Debbie that Rafe was a worthless scoundrel, eventually they quit commenting. The woman had sucked up every ounce of sympathy she was going to get and would be better off moving on to a different whipping boy. Even scrolling back years showed no mention of Fiona. Hard to know what happened between the family members to cause that type of reaction. She assumed Marilyn, Fiona's mother, had lived in Texas and moved to Indianapolis when she married. Nothing there. An entire night wasted shifting through another woman's bitterness.

Max stretched, yawned and padded over to lick her hand, which was a clear indication he wanted to go outside. At important times, such as the need to pee, her dog could be very low key.

As she stood at the open door watching Max, Karly bustled around behind her. The coffee aroma wafted her way, causing her to close her eyes and inhale gratefully. Coffee. It's what she needed to get started, especially considering she spent the night napping on her keyboard. There might not have been any alternative accommodations considering the house was bare bones when compared with the luxurious kennel. Fiona was definitely not a Taurus who valued her personal comforts.

Her dog, instead of doing what he should do, strolled around the yard sniffing everything. Every now and then, he'd pause, cock his head as if considering the spot, then move on. Even though she considered yelling, she didn't. It would only annoy Max who would make a point of taking longer. She'd made the mistake of mentioning the dog's passive aggressive tendencies to Karly who laughed it off and told her she was imagining things. Maybe she was.

Something at the edge of her memory teased her. There was something she needed to do. The morning light was still low on the horizon, but it was visible, which meant it had to be around eight. Her eyelids popped open as wide as they could go.

"Oh sugar cookies!" She abandoned her place at the door, leaving it open to search for her phone. Where had she put it? Nala pawed through the stacked papers on the table without success. The object of her search buzzed and chirped, leading her to the trashcan by the table. Underneath several yellow legal paper wads, sat her phone.

After swiping right, she answered, hoping for a call about Fiona.

"Hello."

"Ms. Bonne, are you planning to come into work today? The children arrived to a dark classroom. Do you realize how traumatic that can be on their fragile psyches?"

Ah yes, her preschool job. That's what she'd forgotten. If she'd gone online and used Subfinder, she wouldn't have to talk to anyone and fake an illness. Just her luck, the principal, who knew she had no great love for her job, would call. He'd naturally be suspicious of any excuse she'd give. Since she already answered the phone and sounded reasonably healthy, she needed a different angle.

What she needed was to push out a legitimate sob. The idea of dealing with two of her darlings who weren't successfully potty trained and the third who was a sociopath in the making created a tiny whimper that sounded more like a kitten mewling.

"My aunt died last night." It was an inspired excuse as long as she kept the details vague. Connie, the kindergarten teacher across the hall, reported that the principal had her bring in her mother's obituary. That would be tricky since none of the recently departed would mention her family as survivors.

"Sorry to hear that, but the funeral won't be today. We need you in the classroom now. I had to send my secretary down to cover the class."

That explained why the secretary didn't call. "I'd love to do that, but my aunt lived in Texas, and we have to drive down there. It takes a while," She improvised the best she could. What place was far enough away to take a long time to get there? "Galveston."

"You should fly. We can't spare you that long. Come in, get some plans together, and I'll do my best to get a sub, which won't be easy because you know women today."

No, she didn't want to hear about how women didn't want to

work with preschoolers. Why didn't he ever call a man? Maybe there was an unemployed male teacher praying for a job.

"Okay, I'll be there as soon as I can." She hung up without saying goodbye. It would take her forever to get to school, especially if she had to drop Max off at the house first.

Karly brought her a mug of coffee and placed it on the table. Nala turned to pick it up and her friend giggled. It was nice someone could find humor in the day that started out crappy and showed all signs of getting worse. "What's so funny?"

"Your face." She reached out and dusted her fingers across Nala's cheek. "Go look in the mirror."

Almost afraid to, she ducked into the bathroom. Her eyes were still a bit fuzzy with sleep, but she could see the indents the keys had made on her face. Each key had Braille symbols that made it easy for the blind to type. Yeah, she looked like the losing end of the fight or the recipient of some bizarre computer virus that made the transition to humans. What she didn't look like was a grieving niece. She turned on the tap and splashed cold water on her face, hoping it would diminish the marks.

She padded out of the bathroom and met her friend in the hall. "I look awful, and I have to go into school, because I forgot to call in last night. I didn't bring anything with me." She gestured to her wrinkled outfit. "I wore this yesterday." She turned her head a little to sniff her shoulder. "It smells, too."

"That stinks. Not you, your job. I have some extra clothes in my car. You never know in the shelter when you'll need to change. You jump in the shower, and I'll go get them."

Nala sighed. The universe was conspiring to get her to work. Since she didn't have a trust fund or a boatload of cases she'd have to do her part, too. At least, in the shower, she usually came up with her best ideas.

Unknown showers usually provided you with freezing or scalding water for those who were trusting enough to get in immediately and turn them on. No, thank you, she'd already had her share of unpleasant surprises. She turned on the water to give it time to warm up. Once the water was bearable, she shucked her clothes and stepped into the shower, placing her feet on the non-skid dog appliques. Fiona had a dog breeds of the world shower curtain. Maybe not all the breeds got on there, but whoever designed it made a diligent effort to crowd them all in.

Nala reached for the bargain brand shampoo feeling somewhat guilty using the woman's toiletries. It might feel different if she had more of a clue. Right now, all she had deduction-wise was it was personal. Fiona was not an easy person to like. There was also the assumption she had scads of money, which might not be the case. Since the woman never socialized, there was no one she could tell she had no money to spread that rumor around.

What do you do if you kidnap someone, and they have no one to call for a ransom demand? The simplest thing would be to drive to an ATM and have them withdraw their own money. Only problem with that, besides having the money accessible, is most banks limit how much money you can withdraw. Every ATM has cameras on them, which could capture the face of the kidnapper if he stood behind Fiona.

Well, this wasn't helping her. She lathered up her hair, rinsed it and then reached for the conditioner. What she wanted was for the half-brother to be guilty. He was a natural fit due to being resentful because his father bowed out of his life and lavished attention on his daughter. She doubted if Herman and Fiona had ever met. Plenty of folks divorced, leaving a trail of children in their wake. Some even managed to successfully combine stepchildren and half-siblings into a workable unit. Apparently, the Bridgewaters weren't the closest of relatives. It would make things so easy, but they may have never even met. No lazy Christmas visits where the adults talked in the living room, while the daughter was expected to show off her new toys to the cousins who would break them. Wait, that was her childhood.

While she was on her final rinse, she decided to ask Elvin for some of his computer magic. He'd find an obituary of a female of the right age and put the Bonne family into the text somewhere. She could give her principal a copy, claiming her mother wanted the original. At least that's the way it would work in her story. Currently, she felt the man was not trying to find a replacement since he had Nala at sub pay as opposed to licensed teacher pay. Why would he want to find someone to take over her position? When she thought of it that way, she could accept her own twisted plans to garner a few extra days off.

Nala twisted off the water and stepped on the puppy bath rug to dry off. A pair of clean faded jeans were on the towel rack along with a blue T-shirt that had big dogs on the front with the words, *I like big dogs. I cannot lie.* The back of the shirt was the rear view of the dogs. That ought to make her the talk of the school by wearing jeans and a slogan top that were on the principal's do not wear list. It was marginally better than showing up in nasty, wrinkled clothes.

After dressing, she entered the living room toweling her hair. "Karly, I don't know how long this will take. Could you watch Max for me?"

"No problem." She held out a foil wrapped square. "I made you breakfast. You can eat it in the car."

"That's sweet." She took the sandwich packet to the bathroom where she ran a comb through her locks. Her finger served as a toothbrush since she could not convince herself that it would ever be all right to use someone else's toothbrush no matter how urgent the need.

Ready, she grabbed her sandwich, promising to call as soon as she could. Leaving Tipton, the traffic was a little lighter than she expected, probably because everyone had already left for work. Right about this time, she'd be doing calendar work. The kids would sing their days of the week song that they clapped to. Clapping was such an underrated skill, she had found. No one at the university level ever explained that part of her job would be to teach children to use tissues, go to the bathroom before they wet themselves, and not to eat clay or assorted other art supplies. Colors, numbers, and the alphabet she expected, but she didn't expect to train five-years-olds not to curse.

The school needed the secretary, who often served as a receptionist and had the unsavory job of telling non-custodial parents they were not allowed to take their child out of school without prior authorization, usually creating verbal fireworks. Her foot tapped the gas, not that she wanted to get there any faster. She didn't want to consider what would happen without the school's gatekeeper. The principal would let anyone in since he probably didn't bother to read the parent notes about who absolutely could not pick their child up.

In truth, she felt sorry for the secretary who had no clue what she was walking into. A handful of her kids were well mannered and totally colored inside the lines. They weren't the issue, except for Hannah who would totally take control of the class as if it were her right. She grudgingly ceded control to Nala, possibly only because she was bigger. Maybe she'd showed the same respect for the secretary, but Nala doubted it.

Chapter Fifteen

WHEN NALA ARRIVED at the school, she sprinted across the parking lot, avoiding the office. Her goal was to use her fob to get in the side door. Her gait faltered when she could have sworn she saw a clown ducking around the corner of the building. She blinked, wondering if all this talk of clown sightings was getting to her. Nothing. She must have imagined it.

If any individual decided to don a clown suit, a school full of children would be the last place they'd want to go. Instead of hearing shouts of delight, there would be screams and a few of the braver students might even attack. No wonder so many circuses were folding up their tents. Clowns were the last things she needed to think about considering everything she had left undone. If only she had remembered to call in last night this could have been avoided.

When she opened the side door, she could hear her class. A few teachers peeked out of their classrooms, their faces drawn in equal measures of concern and indecision, possibly wondering if they should intercede. One spotted her and waved.

"I'm glad you're here. I sent the reading aide up to help, but she never returned."

Nala held up her hand, stating, "I'll take care of it."

Her jaw clenched as she heard the shrill voices of her known instigators. Underneath the clamor, she could hear the gentle murmur of adult voices. Most likely asking the children to sit down and use their inside voices to no avail. She could have told them that wouldn't work.

She stood in the open door and watched the chaos for a few seconds. A couple of the children had paint on their faces and another one had glitter on hers. Glitter and paint were in a very high cabinet since Nala had made the initial summation that her class wasn't ready for such advanced art supplies. Apparently, someone had made the decision to get them down.

A few of her better students cowered under a table and saw her first. Nala clapped her hands together rhythmically four times in the agreed upon pattern that called for order. The students were to stop what they were doing and wait for instruction. She did it again, praying for the right response. She gave every munchkin the benefit of her narrow-eyed gaze that shouted her displeasure.

"On your letter now." She pointed to the blue carpet with the alphabet ring that was standard in every lower grade. The children hurried to take their assigned seats, except for Hannah who stood near the calendar with a pointer as if ready to start the lesson.

Nala cleared her throat and pointed to the H on the floor. Hannah reluctantly took a seat, although she took the pointer with her. The reading aide fluttered close to her side while the secretary sagged against the wall.

"I heard about your aunt, Nala. Is there anything I can do to help you get your plans ready?"

Nala had taught the year before, had kept to the same teaching plans, and had her books marked with what to copy for each week. The tiny streak of OCD she exhibited when it came to copying she could thank her mother for. Nevertheless, the first rule of teaching is never, ever refuse free help.

"Ah yes, thank you, Mrs. D." The kids all referred to the elderly woman as Mrs. D, probably because her name was too hard for them to pronounce. Whatever it was she had long since forgotten. "Could you copy those pages with the pink sticky notes?"

"Of course, will that be enough for the entire week?"

The phrase the entire week came with flashing lights. At least it did in her mind. Her fabrication about Texas had worked. Normally, she didn't lie, and the fib did bother her. She attempted to placate her inconvenient conscience with it was for a worthy cause. Besides, plenty of people faked funerals. The gym teacher had more relatives die in the past year than most people had in their entire family. When Nala shed a tear because the man had so much death in his family, the music teacher was quick to explain his one grandmother had died four times already, and she'd seen the same woman at Bingo at the Knights of Columbus Hall looking spry.

The entire week would be four days if she counted today. Subs typically buzzed through work since they usually didn't bother to teach it. Not that she ever had that many subs, but that was the lounge scuttlebutt.

"Do the blue, too."

Mrs. D scooped up the books and rushed out of the room. The secretary gave her a weary smile as she pushed off the wall. The woman left without giving a report on why her high cabinet doors were wide open.

They'd made it through the calendar, counting how many days they've been in school and the word of the week before her most impulsive student, Logan, interrupted.

"Why aren't you crying? The whispering lady said your uncle died. My mom cried when her favorite singer died. She cried so much my dad started yelling."

Nala put her palm out in a halt sign, aware Logan's tale was starting to veer into too-much-information land. "Aunt," she corrected. "People express their grief differently."

The boy looked confused, but at least didn't offer any more details about his mother's obsession with a recently deceased singer. She must have loved his music very much. Another hand went up. She assumed it was a bathroom request. She only had about three dozen a day even though she'd built in bathroom breaks throughout the day.

"Go ahead."

The child spoke instead of jumping up for a restroom emergency. "Is there a giant toilet where you flush your grandmother, so she has a burial at sea?"

Obviously, there had been no deaths in Sean's family, except for a goldfish. "No. It's my aunt. People are handled differently." Even though she knew the children could come up with dozens of questions, she figured they'd be best answered by the parents.

No sign of a substitution, so she went with what she knew would stop questions about all her various dead relatives—a dance break. The Internet was full of people willing to dress in brightly colored outfits and make dance videos for kids. Educators had learned that kids forced to sit too long did not do well. It wasn't the same as the adult chaos on the dance floor facilitated by too much vodka. The children had specific moves they were supposed to make at certain times, rather like Zumba. Just like the Zumba class, there were the would-be teachers who executed every move carefully, the pretty good dancers, and the confused students who would shake an arm or leg now and then.

The video finished and several voices shouted out, "Gummy Bear Song!" One lone voice added, "Please?"

Normally, Nala avoided the song. It hyped the kids up as bad as eating the actual candy, but since her next planned activity was recess, she'd endure.

"Okay."

A shout of delight went up, but she held up her hand and waited until they quieted down. "I'm only doing this because Daniel said please."

The bespectacled child grinned as a couple students patted him on the back, three others shook his hand, and Logan punched him on the arm. The child needed a crash course in social skills since preschool wasn't doing it. Daniel's smile wobbled a little after the punch but remained even if his arm did hurt.

Nala turned her back to the class and typed the song name into the search engine. One girl in a ruffled dress tugged on her shirt. "Miss Bonne?"

"Yes, Emily?"

"I like your shirt, even if it has dog butts on it. My mommy says butts are vulgar."

"Not surprised."

"Are you vulgar?"

"The video is on." It was enough to send the girl scampering back to the group, jumping up and down as the giant gummy bears wiggled on the screen.

That gave her three minutes to text. At their initial staff meeting, the principal held forth on the evils of cell phones on in the classrooms, unaware of how much his teachers employed them. A quick text message could call the nurse or ask for someone to watch the students while the teacher took a bathroom break. It also got someone to open the exterior door when accidentally locked out during recess. Heaven forbid it would ring, the reason she kept it on vibrate in school.

First, she decided to check with Karly. Maybe Fiona could have returned. It was possible she met up with an old flame and spent the night reliving the good times. Personally, she thought if the people-hating woman met an old flame she'd set him on fire—and not in a good way.

Anything?

Nada. No calls.

See you later.

Elvin was her next text candidate.

How's my favorite hacker?

What do you want?

That's not very friendly. Need a favor.

As I thought. What is it?

Find a recent obit. Older female. Galveston, Texas. Death date yesterday.

Macabre

Scan it and add the Bonne family in it.

Stranger still.

Just do it.

This will cost you.

How much?

I'll let you know.

Ok.

I'll need to know the reason why.

Not now. It's a long story.

I'll wait.

Thanks.

You got it.

The Gummy Bear song had segued into a questionable advertisement that had Nala lunging for the computer to shut the screen
down. Who decided what commercials to put where hadn't thought
that one out. All she needed was some child going home and asking
what erectile dysfunction was. Hopefully, the student would mangle
the term so badly it could never be connected to the real word.

There was some milling and chatter from her dancers on the
carpet. A hand clap got their attention. "We're going outside. Grab
your jacket if you need it and line up."

Tiny little bodies darted around her as they prepped for recess.
Normally, their recess was later and only for twenty minutes, but she
knew the playground was empty at this time of day, which meant
enough swings for all who wanted them.

Nala led her straggly line down the hall, turning once to remind
them to put their hands behind their backs like a ducktail and a
bubble in their mouths. Once outside they scattered, allowing her to
plan out her week for the sub. Her charges thrived on routine. It
shouldn't be hard as long as the sub stuck to the routine. The
children may not be able to tell time, but they had an internal clock
that told them when story time was.

A glance at her phone showed only thirty minutes had gone by.
Thirty minutes she could have spent on unraveling the mystery of
Fiona's disappearance. Every minute mattered. The woman could
have rolled her car and be trapped in the wreckage.

She needed a sub now. If nothing else, she and Karly could
cruise the possible routes Fiona might have taken. If her vehicle was
in the general area, you'd think the police would have found it by
now.

An unknown mountain of a man exited the building, causing a
few of the children to turn and point. Before she could remind the
children not to point, little Daniel detached himself from the group

and hurled himself at the bearded stranger.

"Daddy!"

She would have never associated this man, who resembled a former linebacker, as the tike's parent. So far, she'd only met the petite mother.

"Hello." She put out her hand. "I'm Nala Bonne, Daniel's teacher."

The man reached for her hand with his son still firmly attached to one leg. "Hey."

He carefully folded his fingers over hers. She'd give him credit. He wasn't like some big men she'd met who tended to go for bone-crunching shakes. "How can I help you?"

He grinned, transforming what could have been a formidable face into a gentle one. "I'm here to help you."

This is what came from not reading her morning email. They had star pupil day, parent reader day, and 100th day, but none of them were today. "How so?"

He dropped her hand, gave a short chuckle, and shook his head. "Forgive me. I should have said I'm your sub."

"You are?" Secretly, she wanted to shout yippee. Daniel released his father's legs to relay the news.

"I am." He gestured to his son who was zipping around. "I'll keep that little rascal under control, too."

The idea of Daniel being out of control made her smile. "He's not the one you need to worry about. Let me give you the low down."

She cleverly called all the problematic students one at a time to meet their new sub with the instructions that they needed to help him. It worked so much better than pointing. "Oh, I missed your name?"

"Roy."

"Good to meet you. I'm thankful you could come in so quickly. Can you take the week assignment?"

"I can. I'm sorry to hear about your aunt."

For a moment, she was momentarily baffled. Oh, yeah, right, aunt. "Me, too. At least it was quick."

"That's a blessing."

The ability to leave loomed ever closer. "If you're okay with it, I'll go inside and get my plans together while you watch the children. Watch for name calling, shoving, hitting, and the occasional biting or spitting."

"Daniel?" His eyebrows shot up.

"Never. I'll be back in twenty minutes or sooner." Nala waved to the kids, turned to the door, and used her fob for entry. Talk about luck. It may have been her imagination, but the kids were already yelling less than before. A male authority figure with a deep voice could control her class until she returned. Maybe the man would take her job.

In less than an hour, she had the plans on her desk along with the appropriate copies. She'd shown Roy how to use the computer, LCD projector, and Promethean board. Even though she was relieved to leave, she had to show the right emotions, similar to when leaving for a funeral.

"Be good for Mr. Roy."

A few chirped their willingness, while Logan darted from the snack table and buried his face in her stomach. Since he had been eating pudding, she felt he might be using her as a napkin.

"I'll miss you."

She patted his head. "I'll miss you, too." Surprisingly, she realized she would a little. Even in the pint-sized version she seemed to attract the troublesome males.

Chapter Sixteen

K NOWING HER PRINCIPAL would probably stop her and quiz her on how detailed the plans were she gave to her sub, Nala again resorted to the side door. A quick survey of the area showed no flag crew putting up the state flag, no parents idling in the no parking area, and no junior gardeners watering the dying marigolds. It was safe to sprint to her car without anyone raising a curious eyebrow.

Gasping, she staggered the last few steps, placing her hand on the roof as she got her breath back. Wasn't it a couple of months ago she swore she was going to get in shape? After two weeks of attempting what had to be the most impossible workout ever, especially for a non-athlete like herself, she shelved the idea. It didn't help that Max commented when she did the swimmer move that she had legs and could just walk. On the upside, she did have a car to drive where she needed to go. So far in the private investigation business, she hadn't had to run, except for very short distances.

Nala opened her car door, slid inside, and started it. Her goal was to call her father to see what was happening with locating Fiona's car. It would be nicer if Fiona was with the car, but her gut told her otherwise. If the dog lover could make it home, she would have.

The Beetle flew down the roads only slightly above the speed limit, not enough to arouse the interest of any trooper waiting in a church parking lot or hidden behind an overpass. She made better time getting to the luxury dog compound than she had leaving it.

A honk had her friend hurrying out with Max at her heels. As the gates swung open, Karly's lips were moving, but unfortunately with the radio blasting she had no clue what her friend was saying. Nala parked and jumped out.

"I couldn't hear you."

Before Karly could clarify, Max did. "She asked what took you so long."

"Waiting on the sub. Heard anything?"

Her friend shot both hands through her hair. "No. I'm worried. I'm not sure what to do. On one hand, I think I should be combing the area for Fiona. I might know which roads she'd take more than our friends in blue." She held one hand up and placed the other over her heart. "What if someone is just waiting for us to leave to harm the dogs? I don't know what to do."

As an investigator, she needed to look. Having Karly to assist with her knowledge of Fiona would be invaluable, but for her to go along, they needed assistance. It had to be someone who would jump at the chance to help, especially since babysitting a bunch of needy dogs was not high on anyone's list. It had to be someone who could leave work and drive here.

"We need someone to stay here."

"Almost everyone I know is at work." Karly added, "How about Elvin?"

"Ha! He'd somehow use the dogs to pick up women or at least try to. He's out." Besides, she had no clue what his schedule was and doubted he could drop everything at her beck and call.

"Harry."

"This is his busiest time. People need to get their superhero costumes for Halloween." No need to add she didn't feel comfortable asking him. It would imply a deeper relationship than they had. Who could she ask who was dying to help her? "Mom."

Karly's mouth dropped open. "Your mother? You do realize she could end up with dog hair on her clothes?"

"I know. She's fine with Max as long as he stays in his allocated space, which is the garage, the backyard, and Dad's man cave room. Surely I mentioned how much she wants to help."

"I think you said she'd take over."

"I probably did. She can take over the kennel for a little while. Besides, she has employees who can cover for her."

Karly didn't seem convinced, probably because she had never persuaded Gwen Bonne to adopt a homeless pup or kitten. To be fair, since she left home, her parents were taking many more weekend getaways. She had a suspicion they were having a great deal of fun being empty nesters. "I'm calling her."

Her mother eagerly complied and promised to be right there. Instead of being mysterious about the directions, she sent a link to her mother's cell phone that would connect with her GPS. It would have been nice if someone had done that for her instead of expecting her to find a blue mailbox in the dark.

The two of them retired to the house to map out their search strategy. As they entered the house, Elvis was playing.

"I had no clue you were an Elvis fan."

"Everyone loves Elvis, but apparently Fiona really loves him. That's all she has in her music collection. He'd be the one person she'd love if he were alive."

"Maybe." Nala considered it doubtful. "Do you have a city map?"

"Better. I have a county map. I use it more to trace the areas where a dog was picked up. Often, our incoming strays have actual homes. I have several maps stashed at work, and one with me." Karly dug the map out of her purse and unfolded the it on the table and smoothed it out. She tapped the paper. "I start where the dog is picked up and make concentric circles looking for Lost Dog signs. I'm amazed that people will go to all the trouble to paper the neighborhood with signs but not check the pound or the shelters."

What Nala needed was a highlighter. She emptied her purse on the table. Her phone, brush, lip liner, box of bullets, a half pack of gum, and a dozen markers littered the table. She picked out the yellow one and uncapped it.

"You had bullets in your purse at school?"

"Oops!" A surge of alarm sped up her heart but left as suddenly as it came. "Well, at least I left the gun here. I need to load it before we leave."

Karly shot her a worried glance.

"I doubt there will be any gun battles, but remember you're the one who insisted I get bullets."

"I know, but that was for the dogs. Maybe you should leave the gun for your mother."

"No need. Dad bought her a stylish pearl handle derringer."

"Your father is quite the weapons dealer."

"I'm sure he wouldn't like that description."

"No need to tell him."

"I won't."

The two of them brainstormed possible scenarios. Fiona had suggested meeting Karly back at the house. What side trip would Fiona justify, knowing Karly was waiting for her?

"Do you think she could have stopped for food?"

"It would have been too late for breakfast."

"A little early for lunch, but it doesn't mean she couldn't have stopped possibly to bring something back. Any favorite restaurants?"

"You think I know more about the woman than I do." She gave a slow shake of her head. Her eyes rolled upward as she mused aloud. "Did we ever talk about food? Dog food. Compared assorted brands of kibble."

"That's no help unless there's a pet shop nearby."

"Nope. She orders online to avoid people and gets better bulk prices."

"Well, that cuts out restaurants since we don't have any robot run eateries yet."

Her friend tapped on her temple. "Something's coming."

She wasn't sure if there was a tiny little train in her friend's head pulling a thought out of the forgotten memory station, but it needed to hurry.

"Ah, now I remember. Fiona once mentioned she didn't mind foreign restaurants. The one with picture menus. The less English the better. She'd point to what she wanted, pay for it, and left with a minimum of words."

"That sounds lovely. So, we need to look for foreign restaurants between here and the law office."

"Possibly." Karly pulled out her phone and spoke into it. "Restaurants near Tipton." Her gaze dropped to the screen. First one is Pizza Shack by the Tracks."

"No."

"Taco Bell"

"No."

"Luigi's"

"I've been there. The owner is from Chicago. It's so not fast food." What was with Tipton? Didn't they have any foreign food restaurants run by people from the actual country?

"Okay. How about Restaurante Grande?"

"A possibility. What's the address?" As her friend read out the address, she marked the location with a small X. "Tell me the address of the law office."

"Let me check my GPS. It's not like I memorized it." The landline rang the same time as a horn honked outside. Karly glanced toward the hall, but Nala jumped up and raced to the phone.

"Hello?"

A husky voice whispered, "Heartbreak," then the phone went dead. Snickerdoodles, she should have let Karly answer. At least she'd know if it were Fiona. Why hadn't they put some type of bug on the phone? Even though it would have been illegal, she was sure Elvin could have gotten her one. Police wouldn't until they were sure they were dealing with a kidnapper. Remembering her father's instructions, she dialed star 57 and got a busy signal. Whoever it was, might be calling back. She hung up the phone and stared at it, willing it to ring.

Karly entered the hall. "Who was it?"

"I wish I knew."

The horn sounded from the outside again, causing the dogs to break into a cacophony of frenzied barks and howls. Her mother was not known for her patience.

"I'll let her in," Karly volunteered and headed outside.

Maybe she should wait and call back. Too bad Fiona hadn't opted for a newer phone than the rotary that probably came with the house. She was less than pleased with the information she had so far on possible suspects. If she discounted Karley, she had zero. Sure, she had a half-brother who was abandoned in Germany who might feel entitled to the Bridgewater fortune, although, Karly thought rumors of a fortune were greatly exaggerated.

What could heartbreak mean?

Was it a real call or some strange obscene call? Maybe someone with way too much time on his or her hands dialed random numbers and murmured an odd word, then hung up. As she contemplated the possibilities, she considered Herman Hugo Bridgewater. He was five years older than Fiona, probably still in Germany. What if he wasn't and that was who King Philip heard?

She could hear her mother and Karly talking through the open doorway as she raced back to her laptop. She had bookmarked most of the searches she normally used to find addresses and phone numbers. While Bridgewater was a common name, she was willing to bet Herman Hugo Bridgewater wasn't.

Her fingers flew over the keyboard as her mother entered the room. "Hi, dear."

Her hand went up in acknowledgment, but she didn't have time for chit-chat. Her gut told her she'd had a breakthrough. There were three listed for Herman Hugo Bridgewater.

Gwen asked where the bathroom was, and Karly gave her instructions. Nala surveyed the list. One was ninety-two. Too old. Another lived in California and was thirty-eight. Too young to be the half-brother and too young for such an old sounding name. The third one was the right age. Her eyes looked for people possibly connected to Herman. There was Greta Stamm Bridgewater and Walter. Bingo.

Now, where was the man? There was a list of addresses from North Carolina to Kentucky. The latest was in Fishers, the north side of Indianapolis. Odd that Fiona and Herman lived so close together. It couldn't be coincidental. He could have stayed in contact with his father. It was bad enough that his father left him and Greta in

Germany, she assumed, to start over back in the United States. If he had been mentioned in the will, Fiona would have elaborated when asked about relatives. He had to be a person of interest.

Elvin could run a check on him, which would be so much quicker than telling her father. She texted Elvin.

Call me, now.

She could hear her mother talking to someone in the hall. Karly was in the kitchen with Max. "Mom, who are you talking to?"

Her mother exited the hall with her stiletto pumps making delicate little taps. "Oh, I had to call work."

"Yeah, you've been away an entire half hour." She knew her mother could be a micromanager, but she must be over the top when she couldn't be gone an hour without calling.

Her mother gave an airy laugh that managed to sound carefree and sophisticated. Nala was willing to bet her mother rehearsed that laugh. She was sure it came from some long ago black and white movie. Otherwise, why didn't she inherit that laugh, instead of sounding like duck. Was there a laugh gene?

"Don't be silly. I was calling my assistant to tell her where she could reach me because I left in such a hurry I forgot my phone."

No, she hadn't! "Did you use the hall phone?"

"Of course." Her mother parked her briefcase on the table and pulled out a chair.

Nala slapped the table in frustration, sending a wave of pain up her arm. "Snicker-doodles!"

"Watch your language. What is your issue?"

"I think Fiona may have just called, but I'm not sure. I picked it up, and a husky female voice said 'heartbreak' before the connection dropped."

Karly rushed to the table and shook Nala's arm. "What! What!

You didn't tell me?"

"I would have. I dialed back and got a busy signal. I was waiting to try again. I had no clue Mother would get on the phone."

Gwen reached for Nala's phone and tapped in numbers as she talked. "You really need to secure your phone with a password or something."

Obviously, she did. It would go on her to do list after investigating Herman and finding Fiona. Her mother's voice detailed the situation to her father. She hung up with a smile.

"All right, the phone company is on it."

"Thanks, Mother." No need to add her father had already complained about how slow the phone company could be. You'd think with all the computers it would be little more than typing the number in the search box, but that was dependent on a human doing it and sending the results in a prompt fashion to the police. There might be some paperwork involved to validate whoever was asking was an actual officer, too.

"You ready, Karly?" She took a screenshot of Herman's info and sent it to Elvin.

"Yes. Let's hit it." She grabbed the map with a resolute expression on her face. "Don't forget your gun or bullets. I can drive while you load."

Her mother pushed up from the chair and fluttered around the two of them. "Don't go off halfcocked. I'm not sure why you need a gun."

"You have one."

"That's different. It's for protection. I don't intend to shoot anyone."

"Same here."

Karly opened the door, and Max shot through determined not to be left this time. Her non-confrontational friend had tightened her jaw and pushed back her shoulders as she strode toward the Beetle. If they were in a movie, dramatic music would swell, and everything would be in slow motion. As Nala opened the passenger door, Max's vault into the back seat would appear as a graceful arc.

She passed the keys to Karly, who started the car. The closed gate caused some issue, but Gwen opened it after the code had been shouted out. So much for their glorious exit. The car jerked and bucked as Karly attempted to drive down the long driveway.

"You're in the wrong gear. Shift down," Nala order while she typed out a message to Elvin to check his inbox. She needed the information on Herman Bridgewater yesterday. The car jerked, coughed, and stalled out.

"Do you even know how to drive a stick?" She had serious concerns for her car.

"I learned on my grandpa's lawn tractor."

"So not the same. I'm not loading my gun when you're hitting every pothole there is."

"I wasn't trying to. I was in a hurry. I was just trying to help." Her voice trailed off to a whine that threatened tears.

There was a reason Nala did this alone. "First, let me say you're my friend, and you'll always be my friend."

A sob that had threatened to escape did. "Don't say that. t sounds like something someone might say before they die."

"Not going to die. Just have to give you the talk. Dry your tears. It doesn't help anything. You can load the bullets in the clip while I drive. Do not put them in the gun. Repeat after me. Do not put them in the gun."

"Do not put them in the gun" Max repeated the phrase.

"I wanted Karly to repeat it."

"Oh. My bad."

Karly nodded. "I will not put the clip in the gun."

"Good. Push in the clutch and put the car in first gear. Pull the emergency brake. Let's switch places."

Karly followed instructions, then opened the driver's door while Nala did likewise with the passenger door.

Once Nala buckled her seat belt and started the car, Max gave a heavy sigh. "I was worried. I'm much too young and handsome to die in a fiery crash."

"Hey!" Karly exclaimed and gave the dog a less than pleased glare. "Grandpa's lawnmower was much easier to use."

"It probably wasn't a stick."

"Maybe not."

"Put the directions for Ristorante Grande in your phone's GPS."

For the next few minutes they traveled silently, following the instructions given by a robot voice. If the people at the restaurant spoke no English, she only hoped her high school Spanish would kick in, although saying the sun is very hot today or asking for permission to use the bathroom wouldn't help her find out anything about Fiona. Come to think of it, there wasn't much Spanish she could remember.

Maybe she could communicate with pictures the way Fiona did. "Do you have a photo of Fiona?"

"Why should I? I keep telling you we aren't that close. Wait, I did take a photo of her at the shelter when she adopted all the dogs. It's something we do. We put the photo in a frame and mail it to the new dog parents so they can remember the joy of that first meeting."

"That would work. I need to show the owners who I mean in case they don't speak much English."

"I'm not sure how they could run a business if they didn't speak

English."

"Makes you wonder."

Her phone chimed, which had her reaching for it. Karly grabbed it, telling her,

"Remember, no talking while driving. I'll answer it."

"Go ahead."

"Hello. Nala Bonne." Karly answered, then giggled. "What do you mean I sound too pleasant to be Nala?"

Elvin was a riot. *Not.* "Put it on speaker."

"Yeah, I'd like to hear it," Max announced from the back.

Elvin's voice came over the speaker. "Any praise for my fast work?"

The GPS prompted her to turn left onto the main road, which she did before answering Elvin. "Woo hoo!"

"You could have done better. Your guy, Herman, hasn't tried to hide. He's a hotshot marketing guy who has hooked up with one of the tech companies in Indy. He has a good record with making businesses successful. He gets a company on the radar, and then he moves on."

"A driven personality."

"Possibly"

"Stingy?" she asked, recalling her father's handwriting analysis.

"Hard to say. He does like to gamble, and he could be stingy if he lost."

"Do you think he's a pessimist?"

"He's been divorced three times. I'd think he was an optimist to keep remarrying."

"Maybe he married for money. Could be his wives divorced him for gambling."

"That's all possible. I assume this is connected with Fiona's disappearance."

"It is. Herman is her half-brother."

A long whistle came from the phone, causing Max to complain. "Stop that!"

"How many people are with you?"

"Never mind. Can you give a rough approximation of Herman's movements?"

"Why not ask me to get his blood type? It's O positive by the way."

"Fingerprints would be nice. I might make a run by his property and it would be nice if he wasn't there."

"Can't guarantee anything. As soon as I get something, I'll call you back."

Elvin hung up which meant he was already on it. Nala weaved around cars going too slow. Furious drivers honked. No one liked being passed by a bug, especially an older one.

A colorful sign sprouted above a few others announcing the restaurant. Karly gestured wildly. "Here! Turn here!"

"I am."

She parked the car, then both exploded out of it when a tow truck headed toward a white sedan. Nala gave the car a curious back glance and then sprinted to the car to check out the license plate. Max, who had leaped out with Karly, faced a moment of indecision about who to follow, but turned Nala's way and streaked across the parking lot.

The plates read Dogs28. It was Fiona's car, and someone had called to have it towed away. Wasn't going to happen. She stood in front of the car with her arms folded. Max sat beside her.

The tow truck driver rolled down his window. "Hey, lady, go stand somewhere else. I need to tow the car."

"No."

"What? Are you a whack job, or is this your car?"

"The car is evidence in a crime. I'm an undercover cop and this is," she gestured to her dog, "Officer Max."

The driver gave them both a thorough look. "Yeah, he does look like a police dog."

A siren rent the air as a sedan with a police light almost went up on two wheels as it screamed around the corner and stopped by the car.

Her father jumped out. "Nala."

"I found the car."

"I see. We had a notification via the tow company that there was a car matching Fiona's."

That explained how her father turned up in the same place she was. He wasn't shadowing her, but it was still embarrassing. She didn't mind a little police help, but it felt awkward when it was her father who showed up. Nala let out a deep exhale. Her parents did accept her as a professional investigator. After all, she did have a license she'd obtained from an online school. Never mind she did her apprenticeship at her own agency. "Maybe you could get it fingerprinted. I need to check on Karly."

She left her father and Max by the car. Inside the restaurant, Karly was not only chatting with the dark-haired man, but it might even be considered flirting due to their proximity. "Did you find out anything?"

Her friend's flushed face announced she had been flirting. "Ah," she gestured to her companion, "Ramon said Fiona is a regular customer. They assumed she was mute or couldn't speak English because she only pointed to items on the menu."

"She came in yesterday?"

Ramon answered before Karly could. "She doubled her usual order, but stepped outside to make a phone call or something, and she never came back in."

"Her car is still here."

The handsome man Karly had been chatting with raised his eyebrows. "That's her car? I had no idea, that's why I called the tow service."

"You didn't see anything odd?"

Ramon shook his head. "Look at our windows. They are heavily tinted, making it hard to see in or out. Only the door is clear. I would have had to be standing in front of the door to see anything. Business has been so brisk with the farm machinery show I didn't have time to do that."

"Okay. Thanks. Let's go, Karly." She turned to the door while Karly gave a finger wave to Ramon.

Outside, her father stood with the tow truck driver, and a van had arrived with the tech team, hopefully to pull fingerprints. Had Fiona returned to her car? If so, had someone pulled her from her car? A simple touch of the door lock would have locked the doors, keeping out any would-be culprits. It would have been more likely that Fiona stood on the sidewalk to make her call, making her a much easier target while preoccupied with her phone.

She whistled for Max who abandoned her father. The three of them climbed into the Beetle and sat, having no more leads to pursue. "I was considering visiting Herman's house. You could stay here and talk to Ramon since I may or may not be charged with trespassing. I was going to do the looking-for-my-dog routine. Max runs into the yard. I run after him."

"Sounds workable."

"I keep thinking about the word, heartbreak. Let's assume it was

Fiona. What could heartbreak mean to her? Since she wasn't overly romantic, I'd say nothing." Nala held up one finger. "She did like Elvis who was all about heartbreak, romance, and the whole deal."

"True. Didn't he do some song about heartbreak?"

"Let me check." She held up her cell to her mouth. "Elvis Presley Heartbreak Songs." There was one. "Karly, have you heard of Heartbreak Hotel?"

"You mean that hooker motel off the highway?"

"Well, no. I meant the song. Is there a Heartbreak Hotel near here?"

Karly pursed her lips, before answering. "Well, I've heard about it more than actually know about it. We can GPS it."

Her father knocked on her window, which she rolled down. "You girls let me know if you have any more hot tips."

"Okay, Dad. We're heading out now." Nala started the car as Karly tapped on her phone.

"We're only twelve minutes away. Let's go!"

Chapter Seventeen

T HE BEETLE CAREENED through backstreets never once hitting the highway. They went past boarded up houses, defunct gas stations, and abandoned strip malls. Max put his head on Nala's shoulder to take advantage of the open window and spoke directly into her ear. "Looks like we're not in Kansas anymore."

"We were never in Kansas."

Karly, however was more charmed by his movie quotes. "How clever."

"Elvin. Max is an excellent mimic. Watch what you say in front of him."

A neon sign with a cracked heart similar to an oddly shaped sun hovered over the dingy motel. The pot hole rich parking lot told a great deal about the management and possibly the clientele.

"Look at the place." Karly gestured to it. "I didn't think it was that old. It's a mess!"

"I don't think any money is wasted building these no-tell-motels."

"How are we going to find Fiona if she is here?"

That thought had crossed her mind. It wasn't exactly like her car would be here. Suspecting no names were exchanged when guests paid with cash, there would be little use talking to the desk clerk. Her investigator's license didn't open doors or loosen lips as much as she thought it would.

"We're not. Officer Max is."

She pulled into a parking place at the edge of the lot. "Karly, give me my gun and a clip."

Her friend passed over the requested items. Once loaded, she got out of the car and let Max out. "Go find Fiona. You've been in her house and should have her smell down. Go find her. Officer Max. Go. Search."

She pointed in the direction of the building. The dog gave her a backward glance, then dropped his nose to the ground and slowly sniffed the sidewalk and the edge of the doors. Karly started to get out of the car, but Nala motioned her back. "Call Elvin. Tell him where we are. It's good for someone to know."

Her friend held up the phone as if demonstrating she was doing as asked. Nala waited and allowed Max to get about six feet ahead, so it wouldn't look like they were necessarily together. She doubted people who met for assignations brought their dog along, but she could be wrong.

In this neighborhood, a big scary dog would serve her well. Although calling Max scary was stretching it a little. She thumbed off the gun safety when she exited the car, but she knew enough not to walk with her finger on the trigger, which was an excellent way to shoot yourself in the foot or leg depending which way the gun was pointed. Instead, she kept her gun by her leg, hoping no one would peek through the windows, see her, and go crazy mistaking her for an outraged wife. Max stopped in front of a door. That must be the one. She tried to signal to Karly, but she was looking down.

Mentally, she told herself, It's all you now. *Embrace your inner Bad Ass.* As she moved closer, she noticed the item that had attracted Max's attention was a cheeseburger wrapper. Really? Here she was all convinced they were onto something, and her dog was distracted by a fast food wrapper.

Angry voices penetrated the thin walls. Maybe an outraged wife had already made an appearance.

"Just give us the money. I should have it. I'm older than you."

"Well, you don't."

Nala recognized that brand of non-charm.

An aggravated woman's voice shouted. "What's wrong with you? I could shoot you."

"If you were going to, you would have done it by now. You don't scare me."

Shut up, Fiona. What should she do before the woman got herself shot? Max poked his nose into her leg for attention. Nala knelt to be closer to his ears. "We need to get inside. I'll knock. You yell fire. That should get them out."

Max gave a nod as she slipped out of sight to the other side of the door.

Nala knocked.

Instead of saying fire, Max opened his mouth and barked.

"What was that?"

"I think it was a dog," a third voice answered.

It sounded like there were two women in there with Fiona. Where was Herman?

Max gave her a chagrined look, then yelled, "Fire! Fire! Run for your life."

She would have thought there weren't that many people in the motel, but doors opened and half-dressed people ran out. A woman, who had been intent on escaping, froze when she saw Nala and stared in horror at her gun hand.

"Go on, I'm not here for you." She gestured to the parking lot, hoping the distraught woman and her middle-aged boyfriend would leave. They did.

She could hear the movement and the sound of a body falling. The door opened the slightest bit allowing Max to shove his way through. Fiona, tied to a chair, rested on the stain spotted carpet.

A scream and a curse caused Nala to kick the door open wider. She ran in low with both hands on her gun. Max had one woman on the ground and had sunk his teeth into her judging by the swearing. Nala squeezed past Fiona, who was cheering Max on, and held her gun on the second, distraught woman backed up against the wall.

"Aren't you Debbie?"

The woman turned toward Nala and blinked. "Do we know each other? If you're the police, I'd like to go on record that this was all my sister's idea. Walter Bridgewater wasn't my father. I have no claim to his fortune."

Nala could hear sirens screaming down the narrow road. It would be nice if it wasn't her father, but she'd take any assistance at this point. It wasn't like she could squeeze everyone into her car and hold a gun on them. No way she was letting Karly drive again.

A squad car arrived with a squeal and a fishtailing stop. There was the deeper whine of a fire engine. Someone must have taken Max's cry seriously. The behemoth fire engine made the turn with some effort, but braked to a groaning halt. A young officer exited the squad car, ran hunched over to the dumpster where he took position.

"Police! Freeze. Come out with your hands up."

Easier said than done, especially with two culprits. Max still had one sister pinned to the ground. Nala grabbed Debbie's arm, twisted it behind her, and nudged her with the gun to walk. They skirted around the prone Fiona to exit the room. Just in case the officer thought she was the culprit, she identified herself.

"Nala Bonne, private investigator."

"Are you Captain Bonne's daughter?"

Yeah, of course he'd ask. "Yes, I am. Fiona Bridgewater, missing person and kidnap victim, is inside tied to the chair. Max has one kidnapper restained inside. As you can see, I have the other kidnapper secured."

Debbie yelled, "Not a kidnapper. My sister asked me for help. I had no clue this would happen."

Being strapped to a chair, resting sideways on the ground did nothing to make Fiona into a more submissive person. "Lock up the idiots."

Another siren-mounted car screamed into the parking lot and came to an abrupt stop. The young officer acknowledged her father.

"Nala," her father shouted.

At least, he didn't call her princess. "Hi, Dad."

"Do the perps have guns?"

"Max apprehended the one who did. Disarmed."

"Good. Glad to see my training paid off with both of you. Move in, Officer."

The Officer handcuffed Debbie and escorted the still protesting woman to the squad car. Another officer crowded the door and gestured to Maureen who was hitting Max with her free hand and cursing as she did so.

"Captain Bonne. What about the dog?"

Max still had his mouth clamped down on Maureen's arm. Oh, yeah, he had to be told to release. Nala glanced at her father who gave her a tiny nod, indicating she should do the honors.

"Officer Max, release." He released the culprit's arm and backed away allowing the officer to escort Maureen around Fiona, who yelled after the woman.

"My father wanted nothing to do with you. Accept it!"

Maureen snarled something back, but distance made it unclear. Before Fiona could throw any more verbal bombs, her father uprighted the chair and victim. After using her Swiss Army knife, that her father had promised her would come in handy, to cut the ropes, Nala help Fiona to her feet.

Max walked out of the room shaking his head. "Yuk! Yuk! Bad Taste. Why didn't you warn me?"

Her father glanced at Nala. "Did Max just talk?"

"He did." She expected her father to be shocked, but he just smiled.

"That's funny. Here your mother always thought you had no sense of humor. You really lightened the mood there." He chuckled and shook his head. "I may be old, but you are not pulling one over on me."

CAPTAIN BONNE INSTRUCTED Fiona to go to the hospital to be checked out after taking her statement. She waited until the man drove away before she climbed into the passenger seat of the Beetle.

"I'm ready to go home and see my babies."

Karly and Max climbed into the back seat without a fuss, while Nala debated on waiting for the ambulance she was sure her father had called.

"Come on, girl. Haven't I been through enough? Take me home. Isn't that what I'm paying you for?"

Taxi service wasn't anywhere on the job description she made for herself. Still, she found herself caught between what she should do and what her client wanted. Nala slid into the driver's seat.

"I'll drive you home on one condition."

"You want more money."

"No. It's not about money. It's about your well-being."

"I won't feel any better until I'm home."

The car gurgled to life as Nala considered driving to the hospital. "I need to know if you're hurt. Did they hit you?"

"They got the jump on me because I was on the phone trying to see why I hadn't received the medicine I ordered when they promised two-day delivery. I heard the vehicle, but I had my back to it. Someone put a bag over my head and stuck me with a needle. Everything went black after that, and I woke up in that nasty room."

"I imagine that was quite a shock."

"Inconvenience." Fiona growled the word. "If they were any kind of kidnappers, they'd never let me know where I was or even let me get near the phone."

"So, it was you on the phone."

Karly leaned forward and patted the woman's shoulder. "I thought it was you."

"I was surprised I even got a second try. Like I said they were no kind of kidnappers. Totally inept."

It sounded like the woman was back to her old self, which made the decision where to take her easier. Anyone who complained about how poor her kidnappers were at their craft didn't sound either hurt or traumatized. "Okay, Fiona, I'll take you home, but I do want you to see your doctor."

The woman half-turned in her seat to talk to Karly. "You think Dr. Collin will see me tomorrow?"

"Maybe. If you come by the shelter right at nine. After that, he's busy all day neutering and spaying."

It hadn't escaped Nala's notice that Dr. Collin was a veterinarian, but she had heard vets often went to school longer than a medical doctor. Seeing the vet might be as much as Fiona was willing to do. She reversed the car and headed back.

The whys behind everything weren't clear at all. "When Max and I were standing outside the door, I heard one of the women shouting she was the oldest, and she should have the money. What did she mean?"

Fiona gave a derisive snort as she straightened in her seat. "Walter. My father must have been a player when he was young. I knew I had a brother, because he tried to get in contact with us."

"How did that go?"

"I'm not too sure. It was so long ago, but when he returned, he told my mother he had everything worked out. Greta had married shortly after their divorce, and Herman regarded his stepfather as his real father. He was in America going to school and thought he'd meet his birth father."

Nala made the drive back much slower, giving her own adrenalin a chance to drain away as she assembled the pieces of the puzzle that caused the ordeal. "What about Maureen and Debbie, your cousins?"

"Turns out Maureen is both my cousin and my sister. Her mom and my father had a fling, but when he met my mother, he decided he could do better and dumped her, which upset the family. That must have been when my parents left Texas."

"What happened to Maureen's mother?"

"She married some guy who didn't mind giving another man's child his name. Maureen made sure to tell me he was nothing great as if I had something to do with that. T he woman is bonkers. I know people think I'm crazy, but she has me beat."

Nala listened while another part of her mind played with the possibility of a male being involved in this whole scheme. Her father

REQUIEM FOR A RESCUE DOG QUEEN

thought the note had been written by a male. Twinkle Toes sensed male energy, although the fact she was taking the word of a dog who hadn't even been outside felt a little ridiculous. "You don't think Herman was involved at all?"

"Absolutely not. Greta married a man with money. When it comes to money, Herman got the better deal. I did inherit, but there were bills to be paid, including a second mortgage, and funerals. I had enough to buy the land with the house, build the kennel, and set up a small trust."

That was the information she needed and liked it when she could tie things up. "Did Debbie and Maureen talk about any man being part of the kidnapping?"

Instead of answering immediately, Fiona stared out the window for a minute. "When Debbie started backpedaling about the kidnapping scheme, she kept saying I can't believe you pulled your son into this."

"Is the son here? In Indianapolis?" Nala cut her eyes to her passenger who had slumped into her seat.

"I don't know. I do know he made the calls and probably started the fire. The women started fighting about that, which gave me a chance to call the first time."

One perp still roamed the streets. It was also the one who knew where Fiona lived. Currently, it was where her mother was. A smart person would leave the area immediately, but so far nothing the family did showed much intelligence.

"Karly, get my phone out of my purse and call my father."

Her friend did as instructed and passed the phone to Nala.

"Dad, it's me."

"You're not driving."

"I am. I wanted to give you a heads up that Maureen's son is part of the plot. He could be somewhere around here." She glanced over at her passenger. "Can you think of anything that might help find him?"

Fiona grimaced. "I never saw him. At one time, the two sisters argued about the white panel van they were using. Debbie called it stereotypical."

Nala added, "White van possibly with Texas plates."

"Chain-smoker, too," Fiona added. "I was glad he didn't stay in the room. Even when he brought us food it reeked of smoke."

"Dad, did you get that?

"Chain-smoker in white van with possibly Texas plates. I appreciate the info. We know there is a third person who may be the most dangerous part of the trio. No need for me to tell you to be safe."

"Nope." No need to add that she saw what he did, either. By managing to give her some credit as a professional investigator, he still worked in some parental concern.

"Call me when you see your mother. Make sure she calls me, too."

"Will do."

"Over and out."

No need to tell her father that he wasn't on the police radio. He'd probably be doing the call signals long after he retired. Since she'd made the trip so many times in the last two days, the landscape had become familiar. Even to Max, who felt the need to mention everything he saw.

"Cow."

"I saw it."

"Two more cows."

She rolled her eyes. In some ways, Max did find Fiona. She wasn't sure if it was totally accidental and wouldn't embarrass him by asking in front of others.

"Giant killer birds. Nasty creatures."

"I doubt they're killers."

"They're watching us. Speed up."

"I will not." Luckily, the turn-off was close, which would pre-empt any instructions her dog might make about making a zig zag path so they couldn't follow them or other nonsense. The fact that Max had a fear of unusually large birds she filed away under useful tidbits, especially if they ever had a case involving a bird taller than a child.

The Beetle bumped down the makeshift drive with Nala doing her best to avoid any of the dips and holes, but not entirely succeeding. Fiona tapped Nala on the arm.

"Can't you make this bucket of bolts go any faster?"

Inhale. Remember she is a client, just an unpleasant one. "I'm concerned about your safety. It would be a shame to rescue you just to roll the car."

Fiona made a dismissive huff and settled back into her seat. "Doesn't say much about your driving skills."

Even though she wanted to reply, she didn't. Nala kept on driving, knowing the day would end as would the case. With any luck, she might even get a free day if she could wind it up quickly. One whole day with nothing to do. The prospect tantalized her.

The sound of barking grew louder the closer they came to the kennel, which had Fiona pressing her hands together and cooing. "My babies are welcoming me."

Nala bit back the desire to say if you have that many dogs in one place, there is bound to be one or two barking. No matter how difficult the woman could be, she did love her dogs. It could be a case of her becoming difficult to deal with after being neglected or ignored. She liked the idea of a gentler, nicer Fiona inside her hard shell. Didn't necessarily believe it, but it still resonated.

A trio of beeps at the locked gate had her mother emerging from the kennel with a notebook. Gwen weaved through the rough terrain in her classic heels avoiding rocks, holes, and other obstacles.

Fiona huffed. "Why doesn't she just take off those stupid heels?"

It would be the equivalent of asking her mother to slice off a finger. "Not happening. It is part of who she is."

Fiona turned to smirk at Nala and raised a bushy eyebrow as she spoke. "That's the kind of nonsense you avoid when you work at home."

Karly leaned forward to chime in. "Or at the dog shelter."

Nala said nothing. She refused to pass judgement on her mother who believed in a professional appearance at all times. The woman in question flipped open her notebook and punched in the gate code to slide it open. Fiona had the door open before Nala had come to a full stop. She darted past Gwen who had pasted on her customer smile and had her hand out.

Her mother turned to stare after the woman who disappeared into the kennel. It had to be possibly the only time someone ignored Gwen Bonne in favor of dogs. Karly and Max tried to exit the passenger side since Fiona had left the door open. It resulted in the two of them being momentarily stuck until Nala put her hand on Max's rear and pushed.

The canine tumbled out, but turned to face Nala. "Watch the hands next time."

"You were stuck."

"I know. I always wanted to say that after hearing it on TV."

Nala settled for a nod, wondering how much influence Elvin had on her dog. You'd think she'd be the principal role model, but she wasn't. Still, if she looked past all Elvin's posturing, he could be a dependable guy.

After exiting the car, she stood and stretched. It would be great to go home, eat, get a shower, and sleep for twelve hours, not necessarily in that order. Before she could, she needed to make sure everything was in order. Karly and her mother had their heads bent over the notebook. As she drew closer, she could hear her mother speaking.

"There have been studies on creating a more relaxing environment for animals. Most people think dogs can't see in color. I believe they can. I've come up with some ideas that would make the kennel more pleasing for its occupants."

Leave it to her mother to find a business angle wherever she went. "Mom, I don't think that particular design boat will float. Besides, Fiona has no money."

Gwen's mouth dropped open, and her free hand splayed on her chest. After a couple seconds of open-mouthed astonishment, she retrieved her book from Karly and closed it. "Okay. Maybe there is someone else who has a kennel that needs an update. I see my work here is done." She brushed dog hairs off her black suit and then looked at her watch. "I should swing by the store before going home, but maybe I should go home first and change."

"Don't you have a suit at the office for such emergencies?"

Gwen shook her head, tucked the notebook under one arm, and grimaced at her daughter. "You do realize people could see me in my dog hair suit."

"Who?"

"Anyone. If I stopped and got gas, someone could see me. If I went through a drive-thru for an iced tea. Worse, future clients could see me in the parking lot."

"Of course, they'd immediately decide how, due to a few dog hairs that are practically invisible, your company would not be the one for them."

"Exactly. It's settled. House first, store second."

Her mother headed toward the house as Nala watched.

Karly angled her head in the direction Gwen took. "I'm surprised you agreed with her, having Max and all."

While there were several things she could do, being sarcastic, or at least having people perceive she was being sarcastic, wasn't one of them. "I didn't agree."

"Could have fooled me. It sounded like you agreed to me."

Maybe she'd just give up on the whole sarcastic bit since it wasn't working for her. It also was too difficult a process to explain to people what she did mean. Most of the time, she doubted her success. More likely, people thought she was recanting whatever she had said previously.

Her father's ringtone sounded.

"Hello, Dad."

"Good news, sweetie."

"Lay it on me."

"I sent an officer back to the motel. The clerk was nice enough to allow the officer to wait inside the room, considering the place had been used in a crime. Anyhow, the son came drifting back, driving the quintessential panel van, and it did have Texas plates. He's in custody."

"That's great."

"It is. You can knock off for the day."

"Will do." No need to point out that she didn't work for him. Often, even when she was much younger, her father would pretend she was a police officer, and she'd reply with the correct response.

The fact she hadn't taken her turn as a cop had to have disappointed him after he'd spent a good part of her life grooming her to do so.

"Your mother called."

"Just now?" She knew her father was on speed dial, but she hadn't even reminded her mother to call. The woman must have had her thumb on speed dial just waiting to close the door and call.

"She did, which makes me wonder why you didn't call."

"Give me a break. I just arrived."

"I'd appreciate a call in the future. Do you have any clue how I felt, knowing you might be in danger?"

Was he really going to pull this on her? "Probably the same way Mom and I feel every time you leave for work."

"Touché. I walked into that one."

"You did. Love you."

"Love you, too."

She ended the call and announced, "I'm hitting the trail. How about you?"

Karly shrugged her shoulders. "I'll see if Fiona needs anything, but I think I've missed enough work. No one can match a potential owner with a dog the way I can."

"You got that right."

"Are you going to call Tyler about the cheeseburger?"

She knew her friend would eventually bring up the subject. "I think I will. Surprised you waited so long to needle me about it."

"Things were a little busy if you hadn't noticed."

"Yep."

"We made a good team. What do you think?"

Here it came, another plea to enter the glamorous world of being a private investigator. "You followed instruction so much better than Max. Whenever I need someone to flirt with cute restaurant managers or load my clip, you're my girl."

Karly held out her pinky. "Pinky swear."

She might need to be more specific before she started something she couldn't stop. After hooking her pinky with her friend's, she swore, "I, Nala, swear to ask my friend, Karly, to assist in any dog-related cases."

The pursed lips indicated that Karly did notice the change in language. Still, if there were any dog-related cases, Karly was her go-to person.

THE BUB'S BURGERS sign outside identified the building as her desired destination. She chose a Friday afternoon, which Tyler had free, or she assumed he had it free. He could be on duty and just taking a lunch break. Afternoon said casual. It also said friends, but an evening meal shared shouted date.

She chose the location because she felt it would be far enough away from Indianapolis to keep them from running into mutual friends. It was also along the Monon Trail path, which was a greenway converted from the old railroad tracks. If things went well, they could extend their time together by a walk along the trail.

After she parked her car, Nala checked her makeup. Nothing had changed since she'd left home. Max had complained so much about her leaving him to eat cheeseburgers with another male, she dropped him off at her father's for another training session. At least that way, she wouldn't worry about her discontented pup. Her father might even fix him a cheeseburger.

Her boot heels made a pleasing tattoo as she walked, but might not be the best choice for trail walking. The type of stroll she preferred would be far from athletic, but more on the leisurely side at the right pace for conversation and shared looks.

After walking across the sunlit parking lot, the interior seemed dark. Even though it was two in the afternoon, diners still crowded the Carmel restaurant. She hadn't been clear on how they would meet. For some reason, she thought she'd pick out his blue uniform. Her eyes scanned the diners and discovered three blue uniforms, but they were all sitting together. Not him.

"Have you been here long?"

Nala pivoted in response and smiled up at Tyler.

"Not long."

"Good."

The greeter guided them to a table for two in the middle of the room, which didn't exactly shout romance. Just as well. She was only here to pay back the burger Max ate. They sat, perused the menu, and gave the waiter their order.

Tyler went with a Not So Ugly half pound burger while Nala chose the Less Ugly elk burger. They agreed to share a basket of waffle fries. Once the waiter disappeared, it was time for small talk. She had practiced various topics, even to the point of writing them on index cards, it was still hard coming up with something that didn't sound trite or forced. Instead, she chose to tell him about the clown sightings near her school, which turned out to be a mother checking on the well-being of her child.

Tyler chuckled at the story as she thought he would. "Where the kids freaked out?"

"No. I would have thought they would have been, but most of them never even saw the woman. Goes back to people see what they expect to see."

His hand rubbed his chin as he considered her statement. "Yeah, I understand. Unfortunately, we get too many calls from people who expect to see exes peeking into bedroom windows and the occasional hockey mask wearing serial killer."

"My father has related more than a few similar stories. I noticed you're out of uniform. It must not be a work day." Nala didn't add that he wore the button-down shirt and jeans very well. She assumed the man knew this already. Good thing she chose jeans, too. It put them both on the same wardrobe page.

"I always appreciate a day off. Even more when I get to spend it with you."

A nervous laugh escaped Nala. Accepting that type of flattery wasn't her strong suit. It made her wonder if Tyler dispensed such compliments to all the women he met.

"It all works since I have an unexpected day off."

"Yeah, I noticed that. Did they close the school down?"

Her face flushed, knowing he'd expect an explanation. She didn't want to explain her faked family death and Elvin constructing a bogus obituary for her. Instead, she shrugged her shoulders and gave him a lopsided smile. "Something like that."

"I see. You're going to be mysterious."

The thought of her being mysterious was outrageous, especially considering her father had taken a liking to the officer and invited him over to the house for lunch a few months ago. She wasn't sure what they talked about but was afraid her odd childhood memories may have figured into the talk. Most parents were proud of their children. Only her father would discuss her first shooting range experience, including her wetting her pants when the kickback shocked her.

"Please. I know you have worked with my father. It's not like him to be close-mouthed about his family."

Tyler held his hand up. "Stop there. I won't compromise my

standing with you or your father by talking. Sometimes the best thing to do is to keep your mouth shut."

"Ha! I recognize a Spencer Bonne quote when I hear it. I'll give you a pass." She leaned back in her chair. The awkwardness she had expected in the meeting had flared briefly, but gradually vanished.

The waiter appeared with a tray of huge burgers that gave off a mouth-watering aroma.

"Here ya go." He put the bigger burger in front of Tyler without asking who got what. Placed the fries and drinks on the table, and finally put Nala's entrée in front of her. "Enjoy."

Her elk burger was delicious, and she knew the smell of it on her breath would cause some grumbling at home. With any luck, they would have breath mints at the counter when they left. They spent lunch chowing down and talking about upcoming events. The lunch came to an end sooner than she wanted. The possibility of a walk tempted, but she wasn't sure she wanted to suggest it, especially if Tyler didn't feel the same way.

Nala excused herself to go to the restroom, but hunted down the waiter to pay for their meals. Knowing Tyler, he'd still try to pay even though she was the one who invited him.

When she returned to the table, Tyler was turned in his chair and stared out the window. He must have heard her because he spoke. "Wonderful day for a walk."

"Yes, it is. Let's go then. I already took care of the bill." Finally, something was working out. No craziness that usually came with her family. Just her and Tyler going for a walk.

They walked out into the sunlight, which temporarily blinded her. A dog bark came from the direction of a trail. It was a familiar bark. She opened her eyes to see Max sitting at attention beside her father. What were the odds of the two of them just coincidentally showing up where she and Tyler were eating, especially a good twenty miles from where she left them?

Instead of being suspicious, Tyler waved and took the half dozen steps to reach the pair. Her father and Tyler were deep into conversation by the time she joined them. Her father handed the leash to Nala.

The four of them explored the shaded trail together. While the walk was pleasant, she hadn't expected to spend it with Max. It made Nala think about turning her investigative skills into locating a boyfriend who actually spent time with her as opposed to her father. The romantic spark that flared between the two of them must have been all in her imagination.

Max and she dropped behind the two conversing men. Her dog bumped against her leg attracting attention.

Max raised his snout slightly, cut his eyes down the walk, where no one followed before speaking. "Lose the poor me face. Act like you don't care. Your life is fabulous."

"My life is fabulous." Not everyone had the privilege of being life coached by a rescue dog. Just call her lucky and fabulous.

THE END

A Bark in the Night
M K Scott

Chapter One

A GROAN ESCAPED the silent watcher as the girl pulled out a bunch of keys to unlock the front door. The dog that had been sitting now silently stood, his ears alert, his head slowly swinging side to side as he emitted a low growl.

"Damn it." He hadn't counted on a dog. Who takes a dog with them to an office building anyhow? He could have knocked down the girl and grabbed the keys, and finally made it into the building. He'd spent the last six months trying to enter the place.

The few remaining offices weren't open to the public. He'd even donned delivery outfits and tried to get buzzed in. All he managed to discover was no one in the building had water delivered or even a pizza. Usually, he received no reply when he buzzed. It could be that the buzzer didn't work. The building itself was circa 1930s and only the bottom floor was stores, while the rest were apartments or offices.

That would have worked fine if there was an actual store on the first floor instead of empty rooms. He'd considered breaking in, but he'd most likely get caught and end up back in the slammer. Something he'd prefer to avoid since he had more enemies inside than he did out. Now, he'd have to rethink the situation. Once the girl and her dog entered the building, he tucked his hands into his jacket pocket to feel the short length of pipe he'd hidden there. A man had to protect himself, but as a felon, a gun would automatically earn a huge fine and possibly incarceration. Things he wanted to avoid.

Hands still in pockets, he strolled in the direction of Monument Circle. Sweat dotted his face due to the early heat wave. He could have pulled off his sweatshirt, but the hoodie provided conformity that made him almost invisible.

In the center of the city stood a huge war monument reaching toward the heavens as if trying to touch the departed or at least send a message they hadn't been forgotten. He couldn't remember when it had been built—sometime after the Civil War. As a kid, his grandfather had taken him there. With each war, more statues and flat memorials engraved with names appeared. He remembered fingering the names thinking the people only became important by dying. That wasn't going to be him. Nope, he'd had enough of being Toby Nobody. Once he got into the building, he'd find what was his by right and buy that sailboat he fantasized about while doing time. Might even sail around the world.

Foot and vehicle traffic picked up as he made his way to the circle. A horse-driven carriage, complete with picture-snapping tourists, passed him on one side. The harness bells jingled with the horse's movements. He was not sure why a person would even bell a horse. The animal was too large to miss. Then again, maybe the owner thought it made the experience more festive. Toby stopped and watched the slow-moving carriage. He'd never taken a carriage ride, never took a gondola ride down the canal, either. Nope, those things were for tourists or people with a lot of throwaway money. Soon, that would be him, as soon as he got rid of the obstacles.

★

NALA PLACED ONE hand on her hip and kept a tight grip on the leash clipped to a handsome black German shepherd mix as she surveyed the building. The stone façade building rose a good five stories, nothing compared to the other buildings looming behind it on a more visited street in Indianapolis. The morning sun revealed chipped parts of the façade and the crumbling entrance steps, exposing the underlying concrete block structure.

"The building has character." She glanced up and down the street, noticing the lack of foot traffic during the early day. The ground floor windows revealed empty rooms inside where light spots on the industrial gray carpet revealed where furniture once sat. "I was never shown a ground floor office or even one with wrapa-round windows." Her shoulders went up in a shrug. "It is just as well. Anyone visiting a private eye doesn't want to be on display. I probably couldn't afford it anyhow. Let's go see *our* office."

The dog gave a bark as if he understood. Nala's straight hair swung into her face as she bent to pat the animal. "That's right, Max. It's a new start for both of us."

Max and Nala climbed the first flight of stairs in silence. By the time they reached the second flight, a young man with a dark hipster beard and arms full of labeled boxes met them.

"Hey, a dog, cool!"

A bark greeted his assessment while Nala offered her hand, then pulled it back as she realized he couldn't shake. "Hello. Do you need any help with your boxes?"

"No, I'm good. I'm sure you're not coming to see me. I'd re-member if I had a beautiful woman and her equally handsome dog coming to see me."

A nervous laugh greeted his remark. Blatant flirting rattled Nala since it was difficult to pinpoint if it was sincere. Extroverts could reply with clever comebacks in a second, while people like herself struggled for an appropriate reply long after the person had left. "Yeah, right."

Instead of insisting he meant it, the man grinned. "I'm Harry Chafant. I run a mail-order business on the second floor. Didn't know there were any other businesses in the building. There are some apartments in use, though. Maybe you're here to see one of the residents."

Nala shoved her hands in her jeans pockets since she didn't know what to do with them. "Ah, I'm Nala, Nala Bonne." *Oops*, she had lost a chance to try out her new name. "I'll be opening my business on the third floor. Max," she gestured to her dog, "and I are going up to check out the office."

"Really?" Harry drew out the word, and his smile grew bigger. "Today must be my lucky day. I'm headed to the post office, but when I get back I'd love to show you around."

"Thanks, but I've already seen the building." Regret stabbed her as she watched the man's smile slip. No good would come out of being too friendly to her neighbors. Even if they did hit it off, eventually they'd break up and she'd peer out her door every time a woman got buzzed in, wondering if it was her replacement. Still, she didn't want to sound unfriendly. She held up one hand. "See ya around."

"Yeah," Harry agreed and continued to descend the stairs.

If her best friend, Karly, had witnessed the scene, she'd take Nala to task, telling her she shot down another perfectly good prospect. Maybe she had, but she also avoided a messy emotional entanglement and the possibility of placing another crack in her heart. Some women threw themselves into the dating game with all the intensity of a bullfighter. A failed romance never seemed to get them down. They would just move on to the next guy. The most amazing thing about it was that there was always a next guy. In her experience, most men never passed her father's background investigation test. Oh, the joys of having a father in law enforcement.

On the third-floor landing, Nala withdrew her key to the office and opened the door. The entry office remained dusty and empty. The furniture fairies hadn't appeared overnight, not that she'd expected them to. A few words to her mother would have her scouring the design warehouse for office furniture, but she wouldn't mention it. This was something Nala wanted to accomplish on her own. With helpful, somewhat overprotective parents she seldom felt like she did much on her own. Even with school projects, she had felt they were more a group project.

Her father had built a circuit board that allowed an electrical circuit to run several items at once for the science fair. She, however, had wanted to grow plants and play music to them. When she didn't ace the science fair, her father demanded to know if the fair was fixed. It was obvious the circuit board was the superior project. Her petite teacher went toe to toe with her father and pointed out the circuit board was beyond the ability of a seven-year-old. A third-grader won with an experiment that showed tomato plants grew taller with regular shots of diet cola.

"Let's hit it." Nala dropped the leash and allowed Max to wander at will while she withdrew window cleaner, a rag, and some press-on letters. Her first project would be the exterior door.

"I'm not sure about the clear glass. If a person wants privacy they don't want everyone and their cousin peering in at them as they come to me to consult about a philandering husband or wife."

"Do people even do that anymore? I just thought they divorced, divvied up the stuff, and sometimes offloaded the family pet to a friend, relative, or took him for a ride in the country."

Nala blinked, knowing good and well no one else was in the office. She dropped her gaze to Max, who had his head cocked as if waiting for her answer. *No, it couldn't be.* Dogs didn't talk, at least not in a raspy baritone. She pinched herself just to be certain she wasn't dreaming. It hurt. *Maybe she just thought he said something. The best thing would be to test out her theory.* "Did your last owners divorce?"

Something must have happened to Max since she had picked him up at an animal shelter the day before he would have been put down. Grown dogs were only kept for a few days at the most. Then again, it could be she wanted Max to talk so she'd have someone to converse with. A fellow traveler in this new life she'd plotted out for herself.

"Nope." He grimaced, showing his teeth. "I made the mistake of talking again. Not the first time I've been ousted from a comfortable home. This last time I was driven from the house by my former owner holding a crucifix and calling me *devil dog.*"

"Weird." She shook her head hard still not convinced she wasn't dreaming. I would have thought someone would have put you on the David Letterman show. Whoops, I keep forgetting he retired." *Was she really having a conversation with her dog?*

"You'd think that." He barked a couple of times before continuing. "You gotta remember English is my third language and some things don't translate."

"You speak three languages?"

He lifted his nose with pride. "I do. Dog, of course, the silent language of scent, and I'm reasonably conversant in English. One potential owner tried to speak to me in German. Despite my muddied bloodlines, I couldn't understand a word he said. I wanted to tell him I was born in America. I didn't, since I wasn't totally sure."

"Ah, of course." She nodded her head as if she understood. *Was there anything understandable about a talking dog?* "So, when did you start talking? Are there a lot of talking dogs out there?"

His nose dropped as he stretched out and laid his head on his paws. "All dogs talk in the accepted canine dialect, except for basenjis who do this strange yodeling thing. I haven't met one who speaks English, although most do understand it very well. They might pretend not to know phrases such as stay off the couch, not for you, or not now. They do. Even though they understand English, they freak out when I say something. Something about it being us against them, meaning your kind."

"Ah." Nala searched her mind for how she had treated Max in the few days she owned him. Had she offended him somehow by treating him like a dog? "You never answered how you came to talk."

"Oh, that." He managed a few sharp yips that resembled a laugh. "Funny story. My first owner was a close-mouthed male. Not one to share his feelings or general observations about life. While this didn't bother me all that much, it was an entirely different story for his girlfriend, who happened to be a witch. She always fixed extra scrambled eggs and bacon for me when she visited, so I liked her. Anyhow, one day, she says to the man, 'If you don't talk to me, then your dog will.'"

"Just like that?"

"Took me a while to become a good conversationalist. At the time, I was so excited I voiced every thought." He lifted his head enough to display a doggy grin. "Imagine a constant litany of me listing everything I saw. Tree, grass, dog poop from the poodle two houses down, smells like she likes me. After all, she left it in front of my house. Well, you get the idea."

"Irritating."

"Yep, I discovered immediately that while people yack non-stop, they don't appreciate a talkative dog, especially my first owner who didn't even make the effort to talk to his girlfriend. One day, she was gone. Not sure if they agreed to separate. I just noticed the house smelled less like the sandalwood incense she always burned. After that, I got relocated, too."

"Where?"

"A family with kids. They had a little boy I adored. He wasn't that good at walking so he often hung onto me when he was unstable. It was only natural that I tried to encourage him. His parents were worried about his developing psyche and the dangers of believing a dog could talk. They thought I was a bad influence." Max stood, paced to the hallway and returned to his original place before circling and flopping back down on the floor.

"That's too bad about the kid. I'm not sure what I'll do with a talking dog."

A foul smell permeated the air. "Sorry." Max offered her an apologetic expression. "The Chinese food you gave me yesterday doesn't agree with me. I love it, though. Besides, stress has that effect, too."

Her intention had been to get a dog for companionship. Karly, who worked at the shelter, had emailed her pictures of dogs that would be put down. *Talk about guilt.* Even worse, when they met for lunch, she'd talk about the abandoned dogs, giving them names and listing their idiosyncrasies. Nala pointed out more than once that if Karly wanted someone to adopt a dog it was better not to mention things such as its tendency to rip up anything vaguely chewable or its midnight howling. Karly insisted people had to enter relationships with open eyes.

As if that would ever work. There was a reason woman shoved themselves into shapewear, piled on the makeup, and clipped on hair extensions. Men didn't want reality, and she was sure women didn't either. On occasion, when they needed a reality check, they'd hire an investigator. She'd specialize in date research. No woman wanted to go on a date with an online prospect or even the cousin of a co-worker and end up battered, broke or, worse, dead.

"We'll have to limit your intake to the weekends. Can't have you scaring off the clients with your toxic farts."

A hopeful gleam appeared in Max's eyes as his ears pitched forward. "Do you mean you're going to keep me?"

"Why not?"

"The talking usually scares people off, but Karly assured me you'd be okay with it. Since you're into magic, psychic skills, and all that." His long tail wagged, hitting the floor. The empty room magnified the sound.

"Karly knew? The woman who never believes in too much information withheld the fact from me that you could speak?"

"She never told you she didn't like Jeff, either."

Nala looked up from pecking at her cell with her index finger. "You mean you and Karly talked about my ex-boyfriend?"

Max swallowed hard. "You know, I could be an immense help around the detective agency."

"How so?"

"Scent. I can tell if people are lying or not by their scent."

She shook her head, imagining how well a large German shepherd mix sniffing them would go over. "I'm pretty sure my future clients and suspects wouldn't go for you sticking your nose in their crotch."

"Please." He managed a huff. "I have excellent scent ability. The nose in the crotch thing is something dogs do just for fun. It's a game we like to play with humans. If you didn't react so strongly, then it wouldn't be as hilarious."

Weddings Can Be Murder

M K Scott

Chapter One

T HE TALL PALM trees strategically placed along the Miami shoreline reminded Donna of a former crime show set in a similar locale. Even though it was early morning, many cruisers crowded the deck as the huge cruise ship was guided into its berth. Steel band music played in the background. Mark nodded at the people below them on the next deck. "No one is going anywhere fast."

Heloise spotted them from below and waved with both hands, trying to get their attention. Even though her mother had taken Legacy's best-known gossip under her wing, Donna had more than her share of the opinionated female. She pretended to gaze in a different direction as if missing the woman's flamboyant gesture.

Not easily dissuaded, Heloise cupped her hands around her mouth and yelled. "Donna Tollhouse, I know you can see me! Your mother wants to know if you and loverboy..." Fortunately, the appearance of her mother stopped the ship-wide announcement.

Mark wrapped an arm around her and dropped a kiss on her hair. "How about we just stay on the ship instead of going back to Legacy?"

"It's do-able, but what about the wedding? I'm sure Heloise has already called in the news." Even though any of her family members who were onboard could have made an early morning phone call once they came into cell range, her money was on Heloise."

"The captain could marry us."

"True." They had played with the idea while sunning on sugar white sand beach. The idea of bypassing the pageantry and trouble associated with weddings appealed to her. However, her hidden soft side relished the possibility of using the silver candelabras and cut-glass punch bowl she'd bought previously at an estate auction. "It might be hard to run a bed and breakfast from the sea."

Mark lifted one eyebrow and asked in a mock serious voice, "Have you considered a floating bed and breakfast? It's bound to be unique."

"Do you think I could jack up the mansion and load it onto a pontoon platform?" Laughter greeted her suggestion, but before her fiancé could offer any alternatives, Security Director Ramirez hurried their way. Even with his olive complexion, his still appeared flushed.

"Mark. Donna. Glad I got you before you disembarked. Your neighbor," he pointed back to Heloise who trailed him, "spotted you from below and showed me where you were. The authorities would appreciate it if you'd do a rundown of everything that happened. Just for the record, of course."

Donna made a dissenting sound that caused Ramirez to explain more. "It won't take long. They only want facts, that's all."

"I'll be glad to help." Heloise had crept close enough to join the conversation.

An urge to be mischievous tempted her. Donna spoke, "That would be wonderful! After all, you were there for so many of the pivotal events."

The woman practically glowed as she moved closer to Ramirez, talking as she did so. "Well, I knew there would be trouble as soon as I saw…"

Mark and Donna hurried away. They avoided glancing back, afraid an anguished look from the security director might have stopped the escape. Giggling, they jogged down the corridors holding hands, darting around passengers until they reached Mark's cabin. Once inside, Donna slammed the door and leaned against it. "Woo-wee, that was fun! I feel like a kid again.".

"Yeah, I know what you mean." Mark wiped his sweaty brow with his forearm. "You bring out the secret rebel in me."

"Ha!" She moved away from the door to deliver a playful push. "It was always there."

"Hey, I didn't say it wasn't there. I said you brought it out." He blew out a long breath and announced what they both knew was inevitable. "I will have to go and talk to the police about the case. Without our help, murderers and would-be murderers could walk. We will give our depositions, but there's a possibility we will need to fly back as witnesses."

That would certainly throw a monkey wrench into their wedding plans. Should they even plan anything knowing they might get called in as eyewitnesses? She groaned heavily before speaking. "Why is it always so much trouble being on the right side of the law?"

"Don't dwell on it too much. Unless you're planning on a long engagement, we'll be married before it even comes to court. We might end up missing our flights though. I've already been through the rescheduling thing. Maybe they'll give us a break on fees if we explained we're helping keep the cruise lines safer."

Even though it sounded good when Mark said it, she knew the airlines wouldn't see it that way. "I wish. They might view the cruise lines as the competition."

"True enough. Did you put your bag out last night for disembarking?"

The dear, sweet man thought she had only one bag. "Yep, but I still have my carry-on and my tote bag. So, if we get stuck in Miami..." She splayed her hand against her chest as if the idea horrified her. "...I can get by." Personally, she wouldn't mind another day, just her and Mark. Half of the cruise Mark had missed while she was busy being Janice's wing woman and the other half was spent on fingering the killer. Not exactly what she'd call a restful vacation. It would be less stress to get back to the inn.

"Everything I have, except for my sports coat, wallet, passport and airline tickets, should already be on their way to the airport."

While this was her first cruise, she seriously doubted the luggage went to the airport. "Don't worry about it. I met a lady at midnight bingo who always uses a bright yellow suitcase since they line up the suitcases where you came on." Remembering Mark's entry through the Puerto Rican Port Authority, she corrected, "I meant where I came on. Anyhow, the woman joked about people with black suitcases often snag the wrong one."

A pained expression knitted Mark's eyebrows together briefly as he lamented. "I have a black suitcase."

"Oh!" She hadn't thought of that, but men tended to go for the nondescript bags. "Well, surely you tied a colorful scarf on it?"

His disbelieving stare meant no color ribbon and material of any kind was attached to his black conformist suitcase. "A whimsical luggage tag such as a shark or Mickey Mouse?"

"I used the tag that came with the bag. It matched the bag."

She shrugged her shoulders. "Maybe when we're done talking to the police, everyone will have picked up their bags and ours will be the only ones left."

"Let's hope not. I heard a couple up on deck talking about staying onboard as long as they could, which appears to be hours."

A knock on the door stopped their obsession on bags and disembarking.

A voice announced from the other side of the door. "It's Ramirez."

When Mark swung the door opened, the man shook his index finger at Donna. "You did a very naughty thing up on the deck. I will overlook it since you helped me track down a killer."

Helped him? That's not at all how she remembered it. Ramirez accepted that an elderly man, who had access to all kinds of drugs, decided to commit suicide by taking a swan dive from the uppermost deck that had a chest high railing. If that didn't have suspicious death written all over it, she didn't know what did. A shudder passed through her body when she realized it could have ended there. All the cruisers may have been a bit put out that a fellow cruiser had the bad taste to die on their cruise. The memory of the incident would last about ten minutes only to be brought up again when they arrived back home.

Before she could correct his reference to himself helping, Mark spoke. "What can we do for you?"

"It's me helping you." Ramirez used his thumb to point back at himself. "You won't have to go through the protracted process of leaving the ship. I've had your bags pulled out of the baggage area and they're waiting in a courtesy limousine. All we have to do is take the freight elevator and you'll avoid the hassle, give your statement, and make it to the airport before your chatty friend." A flash of white teeth signaled a grin, although his heavy mustache overshadowed it.

Limousine could sometimes be code for *aging white passenger van*, but a ride was a ride. She'd beat everyone to the airport, whiz through security, and be one step closer to home. "Sounds good to me. We'll need to stop by my room and get my bags."

Ramirez held up one hand. "Done. Your kind roommate passed them out to me and they should be on their way to the limo."

Because the man was being super accommodating, Donna's antennae went up. People weren't that nice without reason, which made her wonder what Ramirez's angle was. Mark would probably advise her to wait and see and to stop being so cynical. It's hard to make plans if you don't know what type of ground you're standing on. The best way to deal with the unknown was full speed.

Her lips tipped up into a forced sweet smile that made Mark wince the tiniest bit. "You're being awfully nice to us. Fast checkout, limousine, which is appreciated, which brings me to, what do you want?"

Mark coughed, patting his chest as if all the air in his lungs had just been sucked out. Her eyes stayed on her fiancé and judging by the lack of sweating and redness, she deduced it was nothing more than a distraction.

"A woman who speaks her mind." Ramirez slapped Mark on the back. "You've found yourself a treasure."

After clearing his throat noisily, possibly to make a coughing fit appear more legit, he responded, "I often tell myself that."

She doubted that. There was a good chance the men would waste time exchanging pleasantries and she'd never get an answer. Donna resorted to waving, which was such a Heloise move and she resented having to use it, but it stopped the men from their pointless exchange.

Ramirez nodded to her as if he'd somehow forgotten she was

there. "Did you have something to add?"

One hand fisted and ended up on her hip. Some people might call it her *I mean business* stance, but anyone who knew Donna knew it was both hands on the hips that really meant business and not the other way around. "As you know, we're interested in catching our plane. To facilitate everything in a prompt fashion, I need to know what you want." She held up her index finger, "If I don't know, I can't give it."

"Ah, yes," Ramirez's hand stroked his mustache slightly, muffling his reply. "It would be helpful if you allowed me to take the lead. I suspected something wasn't quite right while you and your associates unwittingly contributed details."

Before she could even formulate an answer, Mark shook his head. Did he think she'd allow the security director to take credit for all their hard work? What she really objected to was the word *unwittingly*. It made it sound like she was a ditzy old lady, which she certainly was not.

The hand not balled on her hip went up. She pointed her index finger again as she spoke. "First, you should know I am a seasoned sleuth. Mark," she cut her chin in his direction, "is a thirty-plus year police officer, now detective. He has solved numerous cases with many being murders. Truthfully, I think it is unlikely that you would have solved this case on your own. This is what the police will think. Maybe you should say Detective Mark Taber consulted on the case." The point made, she returned her hand to her side.

He continued stroking his mustache, but then allowed his hand to drop. "This sounds workable, but..." He held up a finger mirroring Donna's earlier actions, "...What's in it for you?"

Since it seemed as if she gave up all claim to solving the case, she'd wait the tiniest bit, letting him think he had received everything he asked for. When Ramirez dropped eye contact and turned to Mark for an answer, she knew she had waited a tad too long.

"I'd like another cruise, free, of course."

"A free cruise!" His hands fluttered in the air as if he were ready for take-off. "That's impossible!"

"No, it isn't." It probably wouldn't be an appropriate time to mention she'd researched the matter before stepping onto the ship. Not that she had any plans at the start to ask for reimbursement since she had planned to sun by the pool while various crew members waited on her. What she wanted to be sure of, before booking her cruise, was that she had chosen the line with the least amount of lawsuits filed against it, which she did. "I've read about cruise lines offering credit for a new cruise when something horribly goes wrong."

"That applies to a fire or the entire ship getting sick, not playing at being a lady sleuth."

"You shouldn't have said that." Mark murmured under his breath, then shot the confused security director a pitying look.

"I shouldn't have said what?" The sly, slightly superior director was gone leaving a bewildered man in his place.

"*Play!* I wasn't playing when I hunted down clues. Nor was I playing when I spoke to the suspects. Should I ask what you were doing when I was supposedly…" She put her fingers up to make air quotes, "…playing."

"He pushed his shoulders back and thrust his chin out. "I was conducting the ship's business."

Donna considered mentioning the casual chit chat that the director made with the various passengers when he wasn't hanging out at the pool ogling bikini-clad women, but she didn't. Instead, she changed tactics. "You did help when Maria went into labor. Anyone dealing with Heloise when she was in full rage deserves some sympathy."

"Yes, yes. This is true. I'm sorry for saying *playing*. I misspoke. My English isn't so good."

She had her doubts about the last part since any ship that carried mostly Americans would hire a security director who could speak English fluently, but she'd give him that one. "The cruise?" She raised her eyebrows.

"I'll see what I can do. Perhaps a discount, maybe half off?"

"Let me think about it."

Mark made a face at her reply then mouthed the words, *take it. Honeymoon.*

It would be nice to get away, especially in the winter. "Don't we have some people to see?"

"Of course, right this way." He opened the door as Mark gathered his sports coat and Donna picked up her purse.

They both followed the man keeping back far enough in the hall for Mark to whisper. "You should take the half price cruise. It would make a good honeymoon. This time we can get on the ship together."

"I plan on it, but no reason to let him know just yet. Especially since I have to hold a straight face while he makes himself out to be the hero."

His fingers entangled with hers. "Don't worry. We both know the truth. That's what matters."

"I agree." She gave his hand a squeeze while Ramirez stood by the elevator clapping his hands.

"Hurry! We don't have all day."

Maybe she should hold out for seventy-five percent off. The way he immediately offered the half-off discount meant that it was the standard compensation package. You'd think for the services of two skilled professionals, they could be a touch more grateful.

The freight elevator shot downward without the three of them saying anything. Perhaps the men were thinking about their statements, but Donna had already moved on to the wedding plans. Since neither one of them was getting any younger, there was no reason to plan a blowout wedding. Once home, she'd contact Herman, who was a justice of the peace and she suspected he'd be itching for a return visit to his former home of Legacy. He might even bring some of his friends along, so she'd need to have rooms open for them, which meant the wedding couldn't be during the busy season.

Summer could be busy. As well as Fall when Columbus Days occurred. The entire town re-enacted one of Columbus's ships shipwrecking off the coast of North Carolina. Even though originally Columbus was supposed to have landed on Christmas, everyone agreed that sailing was not a winter sport in North Carolina. Last year, they couldn't even round up three tall sailing ships and had to settle for one cabin sailboat, a smaller Hobie Cat, and Jamison's Motors pontoon boat, which had a picture of a tall ship painted to one side along with the name of the company stenciled across it.

The elevator shuttered to a stop and Mark reached for her hand. Ramirez led them past the waiting people milling slightly as they shuffled their carry-ons behinds them. As they passed the group, a few grumbled about Mark and Donna getting preferential treatment.

By the time they reached a Staff Only door, comments concerning them being arrested for smuggling now floated through the corridor. One lady piped up loud enough for Donna to hear.

"She even tried to get me to buy an ivory bracelet. You know those things are taboo."

The words stopped her. *Smugglers?* Did they look like smugglers? Wait a minute, that voice sounded familiar. Heloise. She should have known. Even though she wanted to correct Heloise and explain ivory was outright banned as opposed to being tabooed, a slight jerk on her hand had her looking up at her fiancé who still had hold of her hand.

"Ignore her. Gossipers gossip. End of story."

Maybe. In the end, it made her sound rather mysterious. Not that smuggling was ever on her bucket list as something she wanted to do. Right now, getting home, seeing her dog, and everything getting back to normal sounded just about perfect. Although, normal tended to be a relative word at the Painted Lady Inn. If all went well, no one would die in her vicinity in the next six months. With her free hand, she crossed her fingers just to be sure.

Discover The Painted Lady Inn Mysteries Series

Murder Mansion

Drop Dead Handsome

Killer Review

Christmas Calamity

Death Pledges a Sorority

Caribbean Catastrophe

Weddings Can Be Murder

Author Notes

A Bark in The Night was written after many requests from the local readers for a story set in Indianapolis. I certainly knew the town and surrounding areas. Many of the businesses and streets mentioned in the story do exist. While the characters and the very lovable Max are entirely my creation.

Come and visit Indianapolis some time. You might be surprised at its several first-class restaurants and venues. I even have an adorable bed and breakfast to recommend too, The Nestle Inn.

Love to see you. In the meantime, stay in touch via my newsletter. Sign up at www.morgankwyatt.com.

Subscribers find out about exclusive freebies, contests, and personal appearances.

If you feel like writing a review, please do.

Reading takes you to your happy place.

MK Scott
www.morgankwyatt.com

www.ingramcontent.com/pod-product-compliance
Lightning Source LLC
Chambersburg PA
CBHW060427180626
46817CB00007B/2705